DIONNE BRAND

THEORY

A NOVEL

VINTAGE CANADA

VINTAGE CANADA EDITION, 2019

Published by Vintage Canada, a division of Penguin Random House Canada
Limited, in 2019. Originally published in hardcover by Knopf Canada,
a division of Penguin Random House Canada Limited, Toronto, in 2018.
Distributed in Canada by Penguin Random House Canada Limited, Toronto.

Vintage Canada with colophon is a registered trademark.

www.penguinrandomhouse.ca

Library and Archives Canada Cataloguing in Publication

Brand, Dionne, 1953-, author
Theory / Dionne Brand.

Originally published: Toronto : Knopf Canada, 2018.

ISBN 978-0-7352-7425-9
eBook ISBN 978-0-7352-7424-2

I. Title.

PS8553.R275T44 2019   C813'.54   C2018-900462-2

Text design by Terri Nimmo
Cover image: (Open Book) © Subjug / Getty Images
Cover design: Adapted from an original by CS Richardson

Printed and bound in Canada

2 4 6 8 9 7 5 3 1

Penguin
Random House
VINTAGE CANADA

Occam's razor.[1]

[1] Look, what follows is all in the past tense, naturally. So much is. Soon, in October, I'll be forty. I hate to begin with this disappointing fact, but what can I do. Better to stop now and think it all over, make an assessment, rather than watch my insufferable colleagues, with only half my intelligence, get further in life than me. I've finally got the space and the time to collect my thoughts. Anyone walking into my apartment can't deny my efforts. Admittedly, to the uninitiated it may look like a mess—but it isn't. I know where every primary reference, every footnote, every chapter, every comma is. I used to invite people over but I don't anymore. There'll be time enough for that after I'm done with my dissertation. Which will be soon. I hate the look on people's faces when they visit. I thought, at first, the look was one of appreciation and admiration—Who wouldn't love books, who doesn't love paper? But finally I understood it was astonishment.

My brother, Wendell, came to see me a year ago. His reaction particularly irked me.

"Are you alright?" he asked when he walked in.

He tried to embrace me. I hadn't seen him for months, so seeing his face at my door I felt elated—an old feeling, a childhood feeling. But when he asked that stupid question, I said, "Cut the big brother fake, what do you want?" Taking in the hall littered with work, he turned back around. He said he needed a smoke. "I might start a fire in here," he said. The thought terrified me, but he was only being snide, I'm sure. All the same, I was happy to follow him outside. First, I do not smoke at my place; and second, I didn't want him reporting back to headquarters any misinterpretations about my work. I have only diplomatic relations with my parents, and Wendell is a far too self-interested envoy. Was it Engels who said that the family (well, he said "the state") will wither away and be put in a museum of antiquity along with the spinning wheel and the bronze axe? Here were my brother and I on the steps of the museum.

He, of all people, I had expected to understand the importance of my thesis and my complete devotion to pursuing a life in academia. But people change; one minute you know them, the next minute they scare the hell out of you. So many things can knock you off your axis. Small things. One day you are orbiting happily and then the tiniest meteorite kicks you off your stride. So this is the perfect time for me to make an appraisal. I have to collect myself. I must collect myself. Why am I here now and what is my next move?

I suppose I can assemble all the explanations I like but it may come down to a simple one. Occam's razor is instructive. There are multiple reasons why I find myself in the situation of not having completed my dissertation; on the other hand, I believe one ought to take stock of one's own bullshit.

Selah

In retrospect, I loved Selah for reasons anyone can understand. First, she loved herself more than she loved me. And this led me to think that I would get some respite from the world, and at the same time receive the little affections I required to complete my life's work: my dissertation.

I wanted Selah to spare me only a few glances and gestures while she took care of her most singular concern—her body. I imagined her thoughts passing over me briefly while she did her eyes or painted her nails red. I believed this oblique affection, like the affection one has for landscapes or animals, would be sufficient for my needs.

I don't require much in the way of attention, you see. All my life I've sat at an angle, observing the back and forth of other people's lives. Even as a child I found myself on the diagonal to events in the living room and the kitchen. I used to sit crouched with my arms around my knees, trying to watch and listen and not be noticed. I used to summon all my stillness to do this because if I were observed, all events would cease and I would become the object of commands to do some job like cleaning a shoe or finding a book to read. Or worse, I would be upbraided for listening in on conversations beyond my years, which it seemed was a sign of immorality. My childhood was spent inhabiting this angle nevertheless, at the risk of beatings and other sanctions. I enjoyed this vantage point because it provided me with a view of the tumult of people's lives without the involvement. And so I perfected this geometry, I excelled at finding just the right distance from actions and conversations. From there, I learned a great deal about human beings, first at home and then in the world where, I discovered, it was much easier to conceal oneself.

Anyone would be forgiven, I think, for loving Selah. After all, in this world there is a shared aesthetic, however oppressive, however repetitive, of loving a certain manifestation of a woman, and Selah inhabited that manifestation. One finds oneself compelled to take part in the aesthetic, no matter the tedium of its repetitions. It is so anaesthetic—well, actually, it is like a hammer and a crowbar, opening your skull and your heart. You can see its manifestation all over the world on billboards—interpretations of a certain symmetry, or to be exact, an asymmetry. Although Selah, I must admit, was not an interpretation; she was the object, the object of interpretation. She was voluptuous, truly. That word—Selah was its owner. A smooth, sumptuous human being. Even-fleshed, tall, athletic, bracing, supple. Her skin, a burnt almond, yet smelled of cinnamon. I do not mean here to invoke the Brazilian writer Jorge Amado's Gabriela, Clove, et cetera. And I don't mean to dissociate Selah, the body, from Selah, the intelligence, in the way that most people do. We are mainly body after all, and the body is intelligence. We turn it into this petty panto-mime of gender, so its beauty is lost on us. I try every day to break out of the pantomime. Nevertheless, I spent hours smelling Selah's right shoulder. Her skin is so smooth there. She didn't appreciate my dog's nose sniffing her, but the cinnamon is most noticeable there, warmed in the bowl of her clavicle. I asked Selah if she rubbed herself in cinnamon. Did she roll around in cinnamon powder each morning, or did she walk through burning branches of cinna-mon trees at night? She looked disgusted with me. Of course not, she said.

Back to the body as intelligence: the body is, after all, a living organism—with its own intention, sepa-rate from the parsed out, pored over intentions that one can say come from the mind. The mind's inter-pretation of the body is irrelevant. The body pursues its own needs and its own desires with fibre optic precision not even yet detailed by scientists. Selah's body, for example, has decided on cinnamon and it has, to my way of thinking, synthesized all of the atmosphere around it to the smell of cinnamon. Or let me withdraw that previous statement. Perhaps it is my body, my olfactory nerve, that decided on cinnamon at the appearance of Selah, and so it collected the smell of cinnamon around the presence of Selah. On the other hand, there might be a third theory unknown to both Selah and me that accounts for the cinnamon. Whatever the truth of this, Selah smelled of cinnamon.

Let me say at the beginning that I do not know anything about Selah. I do not know where she was born, I do not know about her upbringing or her schooling. Nor do I know any detail about her father or mother. Selah kept all this a secret from me—or not so much a secret as she thought it was none of my affair. I would pry and poke around, asking her about her life before me—to which she would give elliptical answers, not filling in the true details. When I inquired further, in that way I have of forecasting that I am trying to dig out a secret, Selah immediately grew suspicious and stared at me like a star from a distant constellation. It was as if she already saw my plan for superficial analysis and found it boring. Selah also did not care that I analyzed her silence in this same pathetic way. At least, she said, there was nothing in the silence except my imagination, so I could speculate all I wanted.

Back again to the idea of the body itself as intelligence: when I made love to Selah—for that is what she said I did—Selah's body was discerning in every (for want of a better word) touch. In those moments she could tell if I was sincere or not in my life and in my intentions. In those moments life is truthful, it has a core, an honesty; it is a plain act and there is no deception. The body then is like a surveillance machine with nerve endings and light scanners, sound detectors and particle analysis. Whatever is transmitted cannot be reinterpreted or taken back. Selah pointed out to me that it was on her body that these acts took place, not on mine. That is, I made love to her, she did not make love to me. This euphemism, make love, is not how she put it. She said, "It is my body that is at work." This statement was at once stunning for its clarity; somewhat embarrassing for me, as it pointed out an unobserved tendency on my part; and truthful. My embarrassment at these words is still present even a decade later. Selah's body was the body at work. I preyed upon Selah's body. Her body was the central terrain and I, like some bird with taloned feet and beak, attacked her flesh and bones. Or I was like a forensic scientist, but a scientist of love, or an undertaker or a surgeon of love—whatever I may call it, I was dissecting her muscle from her blood vessels in my experiment of love.

I thought Selah liked my lovemaking, my attentions to the most minute areas of her skin. It had seemed this way to me until her declaration. I said as much to Selah, in an unavoidably wounded tone. I did not catch myself before that tone emerged and so I foreclosed whatever else Selah had to say. I regret this, but her declaration had confirmed a doubt I always had, namely, What did Selah see in me? Why had she acquiesced to being with me at all? Still to this day I cannot fathom why Selah took me on as a lover.

I am not avoiding the question of why Selah rarely made love to me, but there is so much more to say about her and about our life together that it would be unworthy to dwell on that or to suggest that it was in any way pivotal to the outcome. Selah always told the truth. That is certain. I, however, never truly listened to her until I was faced with my self-delusion. And meanwhile, I always lied to Selah. I thought I was saving her from the harshness of situations. She, to her credit, never believed me. She went on in her own reality. Selah was much better at being in the world than I was. She knew and assumed the conventions of normalcy that I only paid lip service to, which brings me once again to the question of why I was in love with Selah. I cannot confirm that Selah was in love with me; I could never tell. Sometimes she displayed a great warmth for me. She would leave off her preening and embrace me, especially when I brought her a gift of some kind, or when I suggested, desperately, we go on a trip to a warm place.

Once we went to Seville in August. Selah fought me the whole month, but she also picked figs in the mornings and walked through the Sierpes in the late afternoons looking gorgeous. In Seville, we house-sat for a professor of mine, a professor of philology with whom I had taken a graduate course and had become quite close. Selah and I would emerge each day from our house-sit at the wrong hour—the hour when the sun was strongest and all of Seville was asleep. We drifted through the orange-hot streets trying to find a café, the sun baked us, we felt glorious and invincible. Then, finding a shaded resto, we would eat pescado a la plancha and I would drink a beer while Selah examined her skin. I would try to engage Selah in some talk about Spanish colonialism, or the obvious Arab qualities of Seville, and she would barely respond, as if to say, What does that have to do with my holiday? Selah, of course, was right: it had nothing to do with it. My overbearing teaching often leeched the pleasures of the moment. Selah merely wanted to "be." And how could I blame her? I wanted to "be" also.

Selah had a beauty that was unanswerable, unlearnable. After all, what is the response to beauty? I had nothing to offer in response to this beauty. How do you answer the smell of cinnamon? How can smoothness have a reply? What do you do when you glimpse Selah in a far-off store window crossing a cobbled square with a gnome beside her? You see Selah, she is wearing black, she has dark glasses, she is carrying a bag, she is like a sharp dagger or a bolt of lightning striking the air and you are struck in the forehead, you lose sight in one eye. And then you observe the gnome beside her, the gnome who is you, and the gnome is arguing with Selah. "One month," the gnome is saying, and the sight makes you shut up. But the gnome goes on nevertheless, "One month, you cannot give me one month of peace!" The gnome is haranguing Selah and Selah is indifferent, so the gnome shuts up and creeps along beside Selah. Why is Selah walking with that gnome, you remark out loud to no one. Our days in Seville invariably contained a moment like this. Selah had the dissatisfaction of beauty, because of course beauty can never be satisfied and can never be satisfactory to the beautiful. The imperfect is always more rewarding, more active, since it is striving for perfection. So Selah always seemed dissatisfied to me. Though I could be wrong and perhaps it is my probing personality that casts a doubt on beauty. Yes, my own dissatisfaction infected Selah's contentment.

Selah *was* content, I realize now. I came home sometimes to find her singing along with the radio, the sound of some inane popular song booming against the walls. Ashanti, Mary J. Blige and Nelly. Selah would be cooking one of her specialities—the pots bubbling on the stove, the smell of smoked corn, fried grouper, all the aromas I loved—yet I could not help myself, the stupid songs dominated my attention. They annoyed me immediately and I could not resist asking Selah how old she was, and when would she let go of that teenage stuff? Clearly I loved Selah much more than I loved her ways. Though, to take that back, I loved Selah's ways, despite my objections to them. I loved how Selah remained attentive to popular things while I made up theories for them. Selah ignored me. She said how old-fashioned I was, how out of time, how queer. She was right. I know I am out of time. Everything about our different tastes made me question why we were together, but I still ignored this question.

Once, Selah wanted a dog. She hassled me night and day to go with her to the Humane Society so the people there could examine us and decide whether we were suitable to bring up a dog. Selah wanted a fox terrier or an English bulldog or a boxer. I told Selah these were hardly likely to be found at the Humane Society, but she persisted. And I said again, "Hardly likely." In that tone that Selah hated. I told

Selah that her desire for a dog was simply a fad, one that all the people in the city seemed crazy for. Selah agreed. Why couldn't we be ordinary and get a dog like all the people in the city? After many days I was eventually devastated by her logic and by the implied criticism that I held myself above the ordinary. The truth was, the craze for animals overtaking the city disturbed me. I hate watching people walk along with an animal on a leash. Especially people who I know very well do not take care of things, let alone beings. But more ominously I observed the growing population of dogs in the city, and the ubiquitous presence of cats with their watchful lives. Ferrets, too, have become popular. Why would you want a ferret in a city? Just tell me. I'm afraid that creatures are descending from the forests and insinuating themselves in key locations in houses and apartments. I imagine little seams of earth and little lines of ants and little streams of water lilies and lichen. Then after several decades we'll find ourselves buried in those dogs and ants and streams of lilies. I never admitted this irrational fear to Selah, instead scrutinizing only her desires and fears. As with her body.

So we got a dog, though I told Selah I would not be taking care of it. The dog, a boxer, arrived, fifteen hundred dollars (one month's rent) later, and precisely because I ignored it, the dog formed an unwelcome attachment to me. When Selah was close, the dog, which she called Nasir, pretended a childish helplessness, but when left alone with me this simpering fell away and I could see behind the mask of animality a working consciousness. I would lift my head from my book and catch Nasir lying on the carpet staring at me with less than goodwill. Selah swore that Nasir liked me. But I knew that Nasir was biding his time for some catastrophic event. I also knew that Selah would grow tired of the walks, the feeding and the cleaning up; tired of the little plastic bags she had to carry to the park, the hair shed all over the floor, et cetera. So I folded my arms and bided my time and smiled knowingly at Nasir.

The boxer lasted six months. When winter came, Selah found a workmate with a cottage in the country who needed a dog for protection. And besides, Selah said, "Nasir wasn't happy in the city, he would suffer, really suffer now with the salt on the sidewalks."

I said nothing. Months later I asked, "Have you heard from Nasir?"

"Nasir?" Selah replied, having forgotten who Nasir was. Selah can't take care of anything but herself. Her body requires far too much time on its own invention and maintenance.

In Spain, we visited the Grand Mosque, the Mezquita at Córdoba, and my eyes glistened with its magnificence, its light; my own body shone with the whole of its history. My legs weakened entering its grandeur. I held out my glowing hand to Selah. Seeing me so incandescent, Selah drew back as if I had stung her. I turned to her, opening my arms, and she said to me, "That is what I want. That look. Why don't you bring home some of that." I had no idea what she meant. She wandered off, refusing to speak, pretending that she was intent on the arches and doorways, examining the floors and eavesdropping on various guided groups. I resolved not to allow Selah to destroy the Mezquita at Córdoba for me. I ignored her rudeness and followed her, explaining this and that to her and receiving no response. Ultimately I gave that up and wandered off by myself.

Of course, then it came to me what Selah meant; I was not entirely dense. Selah thought herself as beautiful as the Mezquita, if not more so. I understand her assessment. She was. But the knowledge that Selah would deprive me of this experience in a fit of jealousy surprised and hurt me. I floated through the Mezquita with a mix of awe and rage. Finally, I stood at la Puerta del Perdón, pausing significantly, as Selah strolled around, knowing full well I was standing there at this door of pardon, waiting.

The terrain. The body. I can't say why Selah rarely made love to me. I can't say if I permitted this or if she desired it. It all falls into the gloom of those hours of sensuality. I certainly enjoyed her hands on my back, my thighs, her kisses, her palm on my belly, her strength. It was the way it was. She was the beauty. She permitted the uses of that beauty, but clearly, judging by her remark, she resented giving that permission. Is permission therefore implied in "beauty"? If so, "beauty" is subjected to licence, always supine to desire. What did *Selah* desire? This is the question that haunts me. I believe Selah experienced her body the way I did, as beauty, as sensuality, as the carnal object. And she cultivated this object—that is, she maintained its look, its emanations, its presence. To Selah, it seems, her body was an object she possessed, and so she observed its uses. Why did Selah possess this object? Why didn't she refuse it, say? I don't know. It's pure speculation on my part, all these whys and wherefores. But this is what an academic does. So here I am. This I know without speculating: Beauty lives in the past and in the future, never in the present. You say, like Selah, *In the past I was beautiful* and *In the future I will be beautiful*. Beauty in this sense is always under construction. "I am never aware of how I actually look," Selah said. And by her jealousy I knew that to be true. Beauty is never fully aware, it rises to awareness and then awareness disappears with the promise of beauty's arrival again.

Once, I unexpectedly saw Selah walking down the street ahead of me. She was unaware of me. This was when I noticed her habit of reaching her right hand out in a subsiding motion. As if all that she was kept rising in her and she was attempting to calm it down. This was how I learned more about Selah—by catching her in anonymous moments. Or so I told myself.

Even though I believe that beauty is always aware of itself, always scrutinizing itself, so it cannot be entirely anonymous. Nevertheless, I observed her once in a photograph; this was after she had left me, some years later. She was as beautiful as ever and also, I observed, lonely. There was in her a loneliness that I had never been capable of assuaging, no matter how much I attempted to do so. It was that loneliness which had made me sad for her and which I had always been certain I could help her with. All she needed was me, I had thought—me, there, with her—and it would pass. I wished I could walk into the photograph and reassure her. I felt a call, an urgency to hurry to Selah and make it well. My appearance would put her immediately at ease, after her initial reticence, I thought. She would be relieved on seeing me. We would remain there in the photograph together or perhaps leave the scene in triumph happily ever after as Selah had always wanted. But, as I've said from the beginning, my own preoccupations, my studies, as I call them, didn't make me completely available to this task in the past. If only I had located this loneliness each time the mask of beauty had covered it, perhaps. And yet, and also, Selah's loneliness was also an apartness, a—forgive the word—coldness, a profound unhappiness. I can't help but think it was her own dissertation on beauty that caused her this unhappiness. She was never enough for herself. Well, who of us is? I don't want to suggest that Selah was always brooding. Perhaps it was I who was always brooding. Selah told me as much. I was the critical bastard. I criticized everything and everyone. This, after she returned home one day with yet another useless blouse, or useless undergarment, that I mildly critiqued. What part of Selah did I love if there were so many parts of her I didn't love? I loved Selah, I insist. Perhaps it was my own sense of perfection that I loved. I'm aware that I'm mixing terms up here; perhaps it's my sense of perfection or, say, beauty, that kept erasing Selah's sense of perfection, kept correcting her attempts at correcting her own sense of perfection. I loved Selah, I insist nevertheless, even her perpetual shopping for items she discarded upon removing them from the shopping bag. I gloatingly watched this ephemera find its way to the bundles of clothes to be thrown away—gloatingly, and eventually resentfully, since I saw my research grant dwindling with each return home, each evening. Selah had a job, but after going through her own paycheque she nonchalantly went through mine. With a generosity I would regret, and an inflated sense of my future worth, I at first invited her to use my account if she was short. I hadn't expected her to take me up on it. Yet, I smiled indulgently and shook my head when Selah appeared with a new shopping bag after dropping off her bundles to the Goodwill Society.

Selah loved walking through the city. Through her I used to receive news of what was taking place in the minds of people on the streets. She was a clever observer of life where I only *thought* that I was a clever observer of life. I spent most of my days shuttling between university, library and Selah. And when I walked home I was always too much in a hurry to get to Selah, or the possibility of Selah. By contrast, Selah went walking after work. And Selah was in tune with the zeitgeist. When I realized this, I would press her each day to recount the experiences of her walks. I became even more fascinated with

Selah. I lost the anxiety I felt arriving home to the empty flat and waited with anticipation. This is how I found out about the real motives of a certain shooting in broad daylight at the shopping mall. The police thought the shooting was drug related, but through Selah I knew that it was about a lover. The two people involved were lovers and one was going to leave the other. Selah had it on the best authority—someone knew someone who knew someone. It was also Selah who told me that there were so many big, empty condos going up on the waterfront because racketeers were involved, Mexican cartel money and Hong Kong money, she said, and bribery and corruption with permits. The developers, the land surveyors, the escrow scandal—all this Selah knew about. She told me of a condo corruption case where someone flew to Seoul with the escrow money—Selah knew a lawyer who knew the lawyer who was charged. She said that the developer had sold a ditch in the suburbs to two hundred people, claiming it was going to be a high-end community.

I loved Selah because she filled in these gaps in my knowledge—gaps in what I know about ordinary life. Selah could speak to anyone, unlike me. My face is too serious, my eyes too probing. Selah has eyes that are conspiratorial and forgiving. She has eyes that offer silence. She would hardly say a word. She smiled, and people told her things about their lives. She would eventually ask them the most intimate questions and they would answer. Apparently, people like to go to intimacy first, not last, as I had unsuccessfully tried. The immediacy of the intimate opens people, Selah said, not some distant prevaricating question or some circling thesis. These only brought suspicion. Selah found fault with the way I spoke. She criticized my diction. She said I was too formal. She said I never asked intimate questions. But I am convinced that people told Selah intimacies because she was beautiful. My knowledge lacked the beautiful in it.

Selah worked exact confessions out of all kinds of people. When I try to analyze the place this skill has in the world—the daily supply of confessions that accumulate and layer a certain city, or for that matter certain years—I can't help but think there is some other force at work, a force that curates these confessions into some virtual museum, while the lives that produce them go on. Or is there another purpose that acquires power through the museum of confessions? If this were part of my thesis, I'd say that these confessions, piling up, one on top of the other, operate to keep people silent. It is counterintuitive but what I mean is this: we are all blurting out confessions with their coterminous guilt while . . . I can't finish that thought, but you see where it is leading.

And so the pleasures Selah brought of the outside world were astounding to me. Selah's smile seemed an invitation for confidences, a well where confidences could be absorbed and refreshed. This strange smile of Selah's was a complicated one; it broke over her face like a sweet water. I had a sense of well-being and of sumptuous richness when she smiled at me. She distributed this smile throughout the city. It was always new, this smile. I never grew tired of it. When I think of it now, I realize it had its apex in profound understanding. That is how beautiful Selah was. Everyone who was caught in her smile thought that they were understood. This included awful people too. Once an awful woman at a party told Selah that she had knifed a man. Selah was taken aback and disturbed by this confession. She wondered why the woman had picked her, of all the people at the party, to confess to. I think it was because of Selah's beauty. The woman thought Selah's beauty would absorb the ugliness of the knifing and redeem her hand. After hearing this confession, Selah didn't sleep for two weeks. I know that beauty is not an ointment or a salve, though I do still wonder how the woman made out after the confession. When I told Selah my theory, she sucked her teeth. "More likely she wanted to destroy me," Selah said. Perhaps. Perhaps seeing Selah made the woman sad and angry at her own destruction and, like many, she could not bear the presence of beauty. But I really think it's the redemptive possibilities of Selah's smile that the awful woman yearned for. Selah is both aware and unaware of its power. Even this story of the awful woman is a pleasure to me; how fantastic and outlandish the city is—and I would never have known of the awful woman if not for Selah's beauty.

Again this made me wonder what Selah saw in me. What awful story had I told her? But clearly that was the wrong question. She did not like awful stories. She loved implausible stories, like the ones in love songs. Was I, then, an implausible story? Selah captured me and put me into a box; it was an implausible story she willed me to execute, but I could not. Or did I capture Selah and put *her* into a box, starting a story she could not execute?

I often wondered what my friends saw in me too— so this was not Selah's problem but mine. I was trapped in my cul-de-sac of perceptions.

I was reading Galeano's *Mirrors*. I was at the beginning. I read the words, "On the back of a blue ox rode Lao Tse. He was traveling the paths of contradiction, which led to the secret place where water and fire fuse," while I was waiting for Selah in the lounge of the airport in Madrid. Selah descended the escalator just as Galeano quoted Lao Tse: "Only thistles and thorns grow where armies encamp." The phrase is perhaps an exaggeration of my life with Selah, but one always remembers the difficult aspects of time. Ninety percent of our time together was superb. One never notices space or air, only the chair or table. But thistles and thorns, yes, thistles and thorns.

Let me confide this: Selah hated my friends because my friends loved me. I spent hours chatting on the phone with them when I arrived home some evenings. It was my way of reliving the day and letting off steam at some incompetent asshole or another whom I encountered in the university or at the student magazine where I was trying to insinuate a little politics. I met with resistance at every quarter as I tried to inject intelligence into that rag. Selah would bang pots around me while I was on the phone, then she would raise the volume on the television, then she would march off to the bedroom and close the door. She simply hated my friends. Yes, early on, I had friends. Until Selah's needs, Selah's moods consumed me. There was Terry Lezama. I always called her Lezama. I liked the sound of it. She loved George Lamming. And there was Jonesy. He loved Lezama and he was doing a diss on the chronotopic events in *Wide Sargasso Sea*. They were in the English PhD program. We lost touch eventually. Lezama went to England, to the London School of Economics. I think she's a banker now. And Jonesy must have gone mad with Bakhtin, because the last I heard he was teaching at the Fletcher School of Law and Diplomacy. Selah never appreciated the solace I received from my long discursive conversations with Lezama and Jonesy. Since I could not believe that anyone would hate my friends, I did not catch on to this animosity of hers for quite some time. And perhaps the falling away of my friendships had something to do with Selah's insinuating. This is typical of me, I have to say. I arrive at matters late. I'm an academic in life as well as in practice. I can only study a thing once it has passed. At the time what I noticed was the rise in the decibel levels of domestic life and Selah's constant moodiness. So I would say to Selah, "Sweetie, are you okay? How was your day today?" Then I would find that the bedroom door was locked. Still, I did not think this mattered since Selah and I were not traditionally tied to the bedroom as a location where something of a sexual and therefore bonding nature happens. I would leave Selah to her brooding. I would make her a cup of ginger and spice tea and leave it at the door. Then I would go back to my phone conversations while lying on the living room floor. Selah was not good at long and deep conversations. That was clear from the beginning, and I thought it was understood between us that I would not depend on her for such things. She did love it when I read poetry to her. She loved Yevgeny Yevtushenko, especially when he said, "Say thanks to your tears. / Don't hurry to wipe them. / Better to weep and to be." And better still when he said, "Bite into joy like you bite / a radish." And I can tell you of her laughter when he got to the part where he said, "don't shake off the large wonder / of your entrance upon the scene." Selah would fall asleep to me reading, and when I stopped and turned the light off, she would say in her sleep, "Read some more." In this way I read to Selah works by Enrique Lihn and Adrienne Rich, Derek Walcott and Muriel Rukeyser. Rita Dove. "I learned the spoons from / my grandfather, who was blind." And Christopher Logue. "Silence and light / The earth / And its attendant moon / Neither of great importance / But beautiful and dignified." I read her everyone I could put my hands on. I read them to her as she slept. This might make me sound wonder-ful until I tell you I had to stop. I petered out, even though I knew Selah loved my reading to her and it was the surest way to maintain her love for me. But what can I say? I grew forgetful. I postponed one night until the next, one afternoon for another, et cetera, et cetera. I became preoccupied with my own life: the way the editor of the university magazine was cutting up my articles, the way the bastard downsized my job in the editorial room and formed a clique against me. And my academic work was like a ceaseless noise in my frontal lobe. So no, I could not put my voice to poetry. I couldn't read Mahmoud Darwish's "Psalm 2," saying, "I want to draw your shape, / you, scattered in files and surprises. / I want to draw your shape, / You, flying on shrapnel and birds' wings." If I felt like reading a poem, it would be Langston Hughes' "Suicide Note." Even this Selah would have appreciated—but even this I could not do at the time. Now I'm a bigger person. We are all small people in relationships. Despite my vaunted superiority, I was a small person. I elevated my smallness in my own eyes. Or come to think on it, it was in Selah's eyes that I thought that I was big.

In my defence, let me say that there is a difference between reading poetry to someone and needing poetry for yourself. And in those dreadful times at my job, and with my premonition of failure at my academic work, I needed poetry for myself, not poetry to entertain Selah. Selah should have seen this. But here I'm taking my admissions back; and I don't want to do that, I won't be accused of doing that. The poetry should have continued. It would've made me a better person.

Back to the airport at Madrid. Thistles and thorns. Selah was descending the escalator, coming toward me in a field of thistles and thorns. Late. She had taken her time scrutinizing every duty-free shop in every corner of that airport. We were on our way home to do more of the same at her shopping malls. I was furious. We were supposed to be boarding, and by boarding I mean there was still a bus to be taken from the gate to the plane. I was destined to look after the small details of that inconvenient time in our life. Selah came toward me, oblivious of time. She smiled her smile at me and presented me with a white scarf with a gold border. Then she added, "Shouldn't we be leaving?" and proceeded to the gate. We missed our plane, and to this day Selah would tell you it was my fault because I had been reading Galeano and forgot about the time. Time was my domain, it appeared; Selah was timeless. Selah always caught me off-guard. I would be on one trajectory of reality and she would be on another. As I said in the beginning, I had assumed Selah would go about her business of being beautiful and I would go about my business, whatever it was. But this wasn't how it worked out. Being beautiful, it became apparent to me, needed not only the attention of the beautiful but of everyone else surrounding the beauty—and in this case, that was me. I found myself at cross-purposes.

How did I meet Selah? Selah swore that it was at a brunch of the Berkshire Conference. She had come with someone she called a "friend," someone she has never confirmed as a lover up to this day. I was giving a small talk on Jaqueline Jones' *Labor of Love, Labor of Sorrow*. Apparently I turned to make a point on my slide and Selah fell in love with my ass. So she said later. And far from listening to my talk, she paid attention only when I turned my back to the audience. Charming, I told her when she approached me later that day with this information. Then Selah informed me that there was a way in which I smoothed my trousers upon standing that was also apparently a turn-on—as was the way my hands moved when I read from my talk. I dismissed this reading of my body at once. But not really. Because I too cultivated my body with a hopeless vanity. I tuned it to an athleticism that I and only I (I thought) would appreciate. I, and only I, was aware of its muscularity, its flexibility and its speed. There was not an ounce of fat on it. My fingers were like limber twigs, like the twigs of tamarind trees. Dry aqueducts ran up the sides of my thighs. Long legged—yes, I was long legged, and Selah's observation was indeed correct about my ass. It was high and noticeable and, most of all, firm. I prided myself on these physical attributes and I could be found running around the park near the parliamentary buildings at lunchtime in a sweat to make sure they stayed intact. My vanity was solely for my own enjoyment. I've never had what they call "body issues." I've always loved my body. I am vain. But it is an esoteric and discreet vanity. I'm the only person who knows about it, I don't project it. I revel in this physical happiness.

You would not know this to look at me, I thought. But Selah had observed it, and while I outwardly expressed dismay, a deep satisfaction ran through me when she did. It must have shown. Initially I dismissed Selah's come-on . . . but here we are. My vanity overtook me and I let Selah into my life. I was in the early days of the dissertation. I'd finished my master's and had already published in several journals. I was the most promising scholar of my year. I was offered major scholarships to every reputable graduate program in the humanities. I had decided on the University of —— with a five-year guarantee of research money and teaching. It was in the glow of this reputation that Selah noticed my ass at the Berkshires. I was twenty-eight.

When I say Selah was, and is, unaware of the power of her beauty, and its extension in her smile, I mean that her smile has a force of its own regardless of the consciousness that Selah, in the contemporary, is. There are elements to the Selah whom Selah cultivates that have effects that Selah may not know about or may not be able to marshal. The trope with all its attendant affects, and these are many and multi-valanced and convoluted, is one that Selah plays in, and it is so wide a trope that one cannot conceive of the entire territory it covers at all times, even if one represents that territory. A trope is a trope but a human being is a human being. So though at times that slippage, that difference between them, was not apparent, Selah was an intellectual in the studies of this trope but not the trope itself. And so she was taken aback by the effects of that trope and did not really know what to do with reactions to it—except to absorb them for a short, a very short, while and then go on to the dissatisfaction of more and more grooming and culling. When confronted with people's reactions to her (and, in effect, the trope), she was astonished on as many occasions as she was pleased.

When I was born, my older brother, Wendell, said he felt free—free of attention and obligation. When I was old enough to understand and when he was old enough to tell me, he wished me good luck in satisfying the hopes of my family. He had been assigned to become the doctor, the lawyer, the CEO of whatever dreams our father and mother had. With my birth he would now be free, he thought, to discover what he would become. I was instinctively resistant to this task, and now my brother has gone on to become the doctor, the lawyer, the CEO of whatever, trapped as he was and clever as he is. I mention this to show how the trope of "son" cornered him. A trope is a trope, and my brother, Wendell, was caught sexting an assistant manager in the company he worked at now and the assistant had to be bought off. This behaviour confirmed my brother's embrace of the trope of masculinity. I am far away from Wendell now, though I feel sorry for him. I only heard through my grandparents in Fort Lauderdale about his troubles. For me, leaving the world of my father and mother was to leave yet another trope. This may seem like overreacting but my parents' drive, drive, drive to be the same, to have the most, to get the best, not even knowing what "the best" was—this drive gave me a rash. My family was like an organic person, my brother and mother and I being the legs and arms and a heart and a stomach, my father being the head. It moved, it ate itself and it birthed itself. An organism. That being said, it's wise to have grandparents, as I did. They would visit every once in a while from

Fort Lauderdale, complain of the cold and leave abruptly. The complaints of coldness would coincide with some quarrel with my father. Wendell and I were packed off to these grandparents in the summer. If not for them, I wouldn't have been able to take a year off between my bachelor's and master's degrees. Yes, I would have entered the PhD much earlier, but back then I wanted a separation between me and academia; I wanted to live in the world, as I put it to my father. He screwed up his mouth into a knot and told me, "Fine, come work at the dealership." This was my father's idea of living in the world. There and then I thought to myself: this man and I have nothing in common and moreover he's a danger to my ambitions. My father saw my life as belonging to him, and if I had been pliant he would've strangled mine for his. I had thought I loved my father, but when he said these words I began to doubt that. I began to lose family the way one loses the epidermis each day.

A year after our Spanish near-disaster in Córdoba, Selah and I went to Ghana. There, I left Selah to herself in the seaside suburb of Teshie-Nungua. We blew through my scholarship money with these trips.

I realize now that with Selah I was pretending to be someone I wasn't—someone with endless resources. It's not that Selah asked me to pay. It was I who insisted on paying. I was overcompensating for my father's stingy ways. I wanted to give Selah what she desired even if her desires were unreasonable and even if I didn't have what she desired. Furthermore, I think, sensing her waning interest, I was trying to amuse Selah and to keep her attention. In Teshie-Nungua she said she felt at home with the ocean outside our door and the vendors along the street. I'm sure that she was really thinking that Teshie-Nungua, unlike Córdoba, did not require my highfalutin ways with my little guidebooks and my enforced visits to museums, and my little facts and pseudo-facts about populations and gross national product, et cetera, et cetera. So I heard the wind on the Bight of Benin scatter away my droning words, "For god's sake, Selah, the per capita income here is what you spend on shoes..." To paraphrase Joy Harjo, here in Ghana we were the ruins. But I was superfluous here on this outer skirt of Accra. Teshie-Nungua did not need a language only I, between us, was fluent in. Selah could be free of me. I confess, she was much more fluent in the everyday niceties, the spiritual and human exchanges people needed and appreciated. I was ill at ease on this level. I don't know what people want. They catch me off-guard all the time. I sit and think, and before you know it events have slipped away. Selah, in contrast, was in her element here. Three tailors came to visit us at the hotel and went away with measurements for an assortment of dresses. Selah moved up and down the streets of Teshie-Nungua speaking to bead sellers, fish sellers, kelewele sellers, gourd sellers, cloth sellers, bicycle riders, elementary school children, security guards, cassava fryers, church ladies, bartenders, taxi drivers and street sweepers. She moved with a swiftness and fluidity, doubling back and advancing, and within the first two days of our visit she was well known among the locals and privy to details of their lives that would surprise their mothers. Again, I can speculate, but I don't truly understand quite how she is able to wring these details, these intimacies, out of people. She was calling the cake seller "Joan" on the first day. A few days later I heard her asking how Joan's mother,

Martha, was doing, how was her diabetes. To truly take in this feat of Selah's, this quick-step flânerie, the magnitude of it, go to YouTube and find a video of the Teshie-Nungua Labadi Road; in this way you will embrace the enormity of her seductions. In Teshie-Nungua, Selah found me non-essential. She seemed to forget that we were living together and had been for several years. It seemed as if I was a mere inconvenience to the life she had always planned to live in Teshie-Nungua with her friends and her potential lovers. This is the type of forgetfulness that beauty has. It begins every day anew. It is rigorous in its viciousness. Selah would rise in the mornings, leaving me in a still tight-eyed sleep. She would shower, oil her body, perfume behind her ears, and pack her Coach tote bag to set off on her day. I would roll over and catch her sandalled feet disappearing through the closing door. On occasion she returned with a forgiving cup of coffee for me from the breakfast room. But most days she simply left for her new life in Teshie-Nungua.

One day, from my lounge chair where I was reading Colm Tóibín's *The Master*, I saw Selah strike up a conversation with one of the musicians on the beach, a boy who made drums—at least he seemed a boy to me. This boy, she told me later, was making her a drum. The next day Selah disappeared with him, saying he was taking her to see what she called the real community. She presented this as if her time with me had been stuck in touristic preoccupations. The boy was handsome, the kind of sun-bodied boy one finds on so many beaches. I assume a certain cliché played itself out, although this acceptance of events sounds more sophisticated than I was at the time. I felt something. Loss. And insult. And shock. There I was, walking back and forth from the beach to the hotel gate waiting and looking for Selah. She breezed in late that evening without further explanation. There was a feeling between us like fine sand, a curtain of fine sand, a distance that made me sad and lethargic. I could do nothing about it except pretend it was not there. I asked Selah how her day had been. She said "Great," without elaboration or embarrassment. She was far away from me. Selah is incapable of remorse. Or perhaps it is I who suggests remorse belongs here, as if it would be suitable. I could never assume I knew what Selah was thinking. I read in her diary once—yes, I read in her diary, "I have to say sorry more often to ——." My name was in that space. Selah found it hard to say sorry. She felt it was a weakness. It broke her spirit to apologize. I find it easy to apologize. Selah thought my apologies were insincere. She said that I apologized too easily and therefore it meant nothing. Strange. Strange. She couldn't conceive of the sincere. It's nothing for me to apologize to another human being; I hate to offend. I feel as if I have struck the person. And that, for me, is the most disastrous thing one can do.

Selah loved the ocean, the beach, the sun. And I loved Selah loving all this. I had anticipated us together walking the beach, looking out on the Bight of Benin, reading our books, turning to the ocean and turning again. I always accused Selah of being a romantic, but it is I who was the romantic. The Bight of Benin is the deep belly of a goddess. Amazingly more than human. Terraqueous, it owns you. It has no relation to you.

I cannot remember what else I did in Teshie-Nungua after Selah's return that day. Next we were at Kotoka airport, then in Frankfurt, and then back home. Several times for several weeks after, an inter-national number called our home. I dialled the number that had been left idly on display. Once, I heard the trade winds over the Bight, I heard the waves lift and fall, and I asked the receiver, "Who is this?" Time passed but the sand-screen remained between Selah and me. Though I am one to forget.

Yes, travelling with Selah ate up most of my research money. I can't blame her, though. I wanted to be in the world. I cannot see how one can stay in one's little place and have anything to say about the world. I wanted to investigate the struggles of the masses everywhere. Though now I see I was only investigat-ing Selah, or probing my own self-awareness, my own vanity. And Selah did pay her own way to an extent. After all, she worked as administrative secretary in the Faculty of History at — University. I was the one who magnanimously offered to pay for or procure accommodations. And as the bills from Spain and Ghana mounted, I grew frantic at the thought of having to grovel before my father or brother.

Selah and I loved to dance at a local club, El Convento Rico. They play Latin music there and I love Latin music. We loved to dance anywhere, as I fancy myself a dancer. Selah thought herself a better dancer, and kept up with the trends and the moves. Selah, did I say—it bears saying again and again—was beautiful. Selah was so beautiful she never existed; no one that beautiful can exist. She is a fiction of mine. We were at a party once and someone asked, "If you could be with anyone in the world, who would it be?" And I said, "I am with her now." Selah claims she never heard me say this, but it doesn't matter. It was said. My love was too subtle for Selah. I love plainly. My love is on the floor. It may not be visible as love. It may look like nothing. That is, it may look like air. We walked around in my love; Selah breathed it in. It is not spectacular. But one notices when it goes missing.

Despite everything, I breezed through my course work and my comprehensives in no time. In fact, the course work for me was minimal. The topic of my doctoral dissertation, though, has changed so many times that my committee was threatening to abandon me. First there was "Gender's Genealogies: The Site of the Subaltern, a Foucauldian Reading." Then I thought of "Exhibitions or Memorials: The Site of the Subaltern, a Spivak Reading," then "Gender and Heidegger's Dasein: Informal Imperialism and 5,000 Years of the Gender Regime." I finally decided on a much pared down topic and reworked my thesis statement. I wrote several hundred pages during these changes, each recording the turns of my mind, but could not get the committee to read them until I had my statement pinned down. This statement had to be put through the system and approved before I could proceed, they said. There's no getting around this bureaucracy. Once that tedium was over, I was still left up in the air by the committee. This has ended up being my fault, and increasingly I realize that no one on the committee truly wants to work with me. I fear they only want to steal my ideas. Added to which—and I don't say this boastfully but as a statement of fact—my brain is faster than the academy allows. I settled on "Political Thought as Outgrowth of Gender Identities," and then I thought "The Mask of Gender: A Fanonian Critique."

Selah had no idea about the bowels of academia. When I arrived home to unburden myself, to rail against the academic tyranny, she sucked her teeth and said, "Well, if you are so much more intelligent, why can't you figure them out? Why aren't you done?" I accused her of a coarse logic, but of course she was right. I haven't been able to get around myself to complete my life's work. At the root of the problem are the quotations and references. One is not allowed an original thought. I asked the committee: Does Derrida keep quoting everyone before him to make sure he is right? Does Spivak have to array around her all the dead philosophers and theorists to prove her credentials for speaking? And finally, there's no reference for what I want to do. Why can't I simply speak without having to have that speech legitimated by god knows who? Selah had to give me these last points.

When Selah was on your side, she would fight for you. Fiercely. There is a side to beauty that is fierce, as I've said before. You don't want to get in its way. It will crush you. One night we were out dancing with friends at El Convento Rico. One of Selah's friends became drunk and propositioned someone. The someone's girlfriend jumped on Selah's friend, and

Selah immediately went on the defence. Selah's friend was clearly in the wrong—but she was Selah's friend and that, to Selah, made her right. I tried dragging Selah off the girlfriend. "You don't allow people to step to you like that, no matter what," Selah said. Selah's friend had a lot of mouth, as they say, but no skills. There was shoving and grabbing, and Selah put her hand in the girlfriend's face. We left the club, walking along College Street, me pulling Selah and Selah walking backward and ready to resume the fight. We had been followed, since Selah's friend continued cursing and challenging the attacker for a block after we left. My major concern was not the scandal, the possibility of the police arriving, the unwanted social territory that this kind of behaviour would instantiate; my concern was Selah's face. What if that woman had gone for Selah's face? I would've had to step in beyond how I did, which was to entreat all parties to end the fight. Selah didn't fully appreciate my position. She gave me a look as if I were a coward, berating me for not wanting to get my hands dirty. No, I don't want to get my hands dirty, definitely not, I told her. I'm always for using reason and argument. I can never understand violence. I find it alarming. Selah said, "Violence is too big a word for this kind of hand-to-hand combat." While Selah kept a lookout for the counterattack of the enraged girl-friend, and the person who had started it all kept up a blizzard of curse words, I searched desperately for an empty taxi. One finally drew up and I shoved Selah and her friend into it. They cheered each other as the taxi moved off, boasting about what they had done and what they should've done. Here I want to reference Gabriel García Márquez' *Chronicle of a Death Foretold*. Selah and her friend reminded me of Pedro and Pablo—determined and set, precipitant. They saw no reason to resist a destiny. Meanwhile, I felt as if I were the whole town in the novel, unable to stop what could come because of my inattention or my disbelief. Or perhaps, if it's not too much of an exaggeration . . . well, it is; I was not Bayardo San Román. My main effort was to make sure Selah's beauty did not experience some disfigurement. Selah didn't appear concerned. She had been prepared to put her face on the line, though she did not see it this way. She didn't anticipate losing the fight. "That girl couldn't touch me!" she said disdainfully when I brought up my anxiety. Selah thinks beauty is a piece of armour, that it will see her through all battles. But I think of the beautiful Achilles. There is a heel somewhere on Selah and I hope it's never exposed.

The question remains: If we were so diametrically opposed, why was I with Selah? Simple. Vanity, I believe. I loved walking beside Selah down any street. I could see all eyes on Selah. No one noticed me until several seconds after noticing Selah, and then dismissively. They thought that I simply happened to be walking by at the same time as they were looking at Selah, that I had no possible relation to her life. This gave me pleasure. Perhaps Selah loved walking with me for the same reasons. I set off the vision that she was in a stark manner. I was always incredulous that Selah had chosen me—even now that I understand her choice as the random and arbitrary power of the beautiful. I'm not trying to say that Selah had no imperfections. I could outline them, and will, but all her imperfections were enveloped in that sinecure of beauty that she possessed. Perhaps my affair with Selah can be rolled into my dissertation; perhaps that is what I am doing subconsciously as I ponder the interpretative, the hermeneutics of our situation.

When Selah told me that she was leaving me, I had a spell of catatonia. I lay on the bed for two days . . . or was it three? My eyes descended to the bottom of my life, it seemed, and my brain felt underwater. I saw my bookshelves lean in toward me and the ceiling was kilometres away. I thought that I was dying. This is an expression, of course. People use it all the time, people who are not dying. So to be precise, I thought that I was losing a part of the way I had come to exist. I only recovered when Selah lay beside me and held my hands. I could feel both her sincerity and her insincerity at once, and I hung on to her sincerity and pulled myself out of the well of catatonia. I promised myself never to plunge into that well again. During my three catatonic days the weather was still and blank; events had no future. I will never visit that place again.

By that point I had lost all sense of Selah's inner life—at least to the extent that I thought I knew it. Can we say that we know anything of another person's interior? The whole idea of an interior and an exterior suggests a certain deception, as if the interior is hidden deliberately from us. So let us say I no longer thought I knew what I had thought before about what she wanted. I would like to be indulged in this convolution, since there's no clearer way of saying it. And now this became my preoccupation, whereas, at the beginning of our relationship, I had thought that Selah was her own preoccupation and I would therefore be required to contribute very little to that absorption except in the ways that I could. I myself had made it perfectly clear, both in my self-presentation and in my verbal representations, who I was and what I expected. I had no hidden agendas. This is the difference between Selah and me. Selah worked by innuendo, expectation, pregnant suggestion, expected interpretation. And when all this was misinterpreted on my part, the result was her complete rejection. When I rose from my catatonia, I decided to exit the trope I'd been inhabiting. To be truthful, I was expelled from the trope. And in the end gladly, though the end was long in coming and long in execution. Why do I lie and say "gladly"? It was horrific.

It's difficult to inhabit a trope; not at all as easy as one is led to believe. If the trope of beauty is arduous to manifest, as I think in Selah's case it was—for it took constant recalibrating despite the basics being in place—then to attend to this trope, as I did, was also laborious. For Selah, I think, the benefits or pleasures that you would expect to accrue from manifesting the woman she was didn't bear out. She was never sure, I observe, as to whether this or that benefit was right enough or deep enough. Perhaps the actual pleasure of the objects—the things she received, the people she attracted—never quite matched the promised pleasure of them. That is, faced with the results, she didn't feel the charge that they were supposed to give, and so she kept pursuing that charge as an addict pursues a high. This is all interpretation on my part. What else is there but interpretation? If I thought that I was the other figure in the trope, then I was mistaken. I was a complete failure at this manifestation. I certainly learned through being with Selah that a trope is always provisional, always held by failure, always "being." I don't want to unravel those clauses; to put it simply, I was heartbroken.

After the catatonia, a refreshment bathed me. I thanked Selah for her touch and proceeded with plans to divide our modest belongings. This renewed efficiency on my part surprised Selah, I believe. Though I hesitate to interpret, since it is interpretation that got me into trouble in the first place. I made a list of things. I gave Selah everything except my books, my notes and my extensive iterations of my dissertations. I gave her the date of my departure. I wished her well. I made no more entreaties. I suffered. I tried to remember that moment of surfacing from the well, how clear and clean it was. The world had goodness in it. I could exist, not with plans or possibilities but with nothing. When I was in my twenties, I had such moments—brilliant moments, where my life was illuminated in its singularity. Selah was behind me as an experience and, in the few weeks we spent navigating each other's absences, Selah's presence was like the presence of a ghost. And I, the "me" at the bottom of the well, was like a ghost too. Such enlightenment can't last long, we can't live in sustained enlightenment, since the world around us is full of the past, and so I had to move quickly into the future. I travelled virtually to another city with my folders and suitcases and my yoga mat, and left Selah to her city. I don't know how all of this affected Selah. I abandoned all questions, all interpretation. I took the salvation of her hand raising me from the well and I fled. It returned me to freedom. Was it Sartre who said we are "doomed to freedom"? Well, I was incandescently doomed. I drove down the highway screaming my own name. I conclude that I can't handle life the way other people, I assume, handle it. I'm not successful at the ordinary, as much as I try. I'm not successful at much; my dissertation is still waiting to be done. My gigs at the magazine where I had written two long pieces about my travels with Selah and the odd article have dwindled away. That dreadful editor sidelined me politically, and it will take some grovelling to get a couple of teaching assistantships.

Selah hated paper. This knowledge should have given me a clear sense of my situation—but no, not me. I took it, perversely, to mean that Selah would grow out of this hatred under my influence. Some would say I had an inflated sense of myself, but I call this courage on my part. A more generous reading would be to say that I have faith in people. What is wrong with that?

I know I have not described the place where I lived with Selah. The truth is I cannot recall the scenes through the window, the view through the door. I can't remember them. Were there neighbours of significance? I don't know. Selah filled my gaze. Have I forgotten these scenes or did they not exist with Selah? There may have been a birch tree, there may have been blue jays; there may have been water outside, though I doubt it. It may have been a river far away. At any rate, there was traffic. I turn these possibilities over in my memory, trying to see the window, the doorway, and I fail. I see nothing except Selah. Even when I dance late at night by myself, I am dancing with Selah.

My only hope now is in an academic appointment, and for that I must complete the diss. Selah was a complete distraction, not what I had anticipated at all. Where were my small affections, my kindly encouragements, where was my solace? All these I had expected to ameliorate the harsh world, as I saw it. Those pages I managed to write, the few pages I salvaged from the disaster, of Selah, I don't even know what they say. I keep them in a small suitcase. But I don't want to return to my petty complaints. I want to live in the glow of my enlightenment. After leaving Selah, I wanted to speed down a highway singing "Crazy" with CeeLo Green, then break out into Whitney Houston's "It's Not Right but It's Okay." And it was these two songs that launched me on my new way. I'm not one for songs. Songs were Selah's purview, but she can't have these two. This period of enlightenment was a gigantic floodlight into my mind. This floodlight washed my former life with Selah—not clean, but discernible, as if I were circling all the events that had passed with Selah but in a different orbit.

I don't want to waste another moment more on Selah. I circle the ideas I circled around Selah, not Selah herself. Already I have forgotten Selah, because I never knew Selah. I understood that behind her beauty was the nervous panic, the tension of that beauty, the uncertainty of it.

When I woke up the next morning, the morning after the well, I told Selah, "I want to wake up tomorrow in a new place, without anxiety, without panic." It was wrong of me to have said this to Selah; after all, Selah may not have seen things this way. I apologize to Selah, I apologize to her beauty, this long after. But still, hold my words even if they are not a reference to Selah the finite. I wanted to wake up the next day, and every day, without anxiety. I want the floodlight of enlightenment to shine its beam on me always. For this I had to take leave of Selah. I sped down the highway like Lewis Hamilton. No, forget that reference. It's not a question of winning and it's not possible to draw a reference here because all destinations on our tiny planet are known. Once I saw through a telescope the constellation Cassiopeia, quiet, distant, indescribably sparkled. I sped toward Cassiopeia singing "Maybe I'm crazy" along with CeeLo Green. Possibly, eleven thousand light years away from Selah.

Yara

I mustn't be sentimental about Yara, but whenever I think about her, even though she had nothing to do with my childhood, I remember my earliest years with its candies and split-pea soups. Why is that? Yara's apartment over the railway bridge on Annette Street took me, strangely, back to the scents of my happiest years. The years when all I did was follow one desire to another. Small desires, like a cup of milk or a handful of sugar or the sourest cherry candy exploding in my mouth. Those years can't be duplicated for happiness. They were brief but they were potent. My father had not become an ogre; my mother had not become a doormat. Back then, my father was still kindly. It was not yet clear to me that he saw my brother and me as possessions. Perhaps a child lives as a possession; perhaps the act of resting against a father's knee or hanging off a mother's shoulder are the conditions of being and living as a possession. My father loved us until we could say no. Possessions don't speak. They are not allowed to say "un-own me." Then, in my childhood, I didn't think of the future— or not in the ways I think about the future now. And I didn't think of the past for longer than a few seconds, the few seconds it took to feel the pain of a fall on my knees or to summarize the look of a bruise on my elbow. All these I recovered from quickly, since my only ambition was the next desire. Desire is like this, always dramatic and always ahead. To have desires satisfied is to defeat the purpose of desiring. Desires are never satisfied and that is why they are called desires and not satisfactions. If I thought of the future back then it was only in terms of my desires, not in terms of "a life," let us say. The present was full of desire and therefore full of ups and downs.

That's how Yara was—full of ups and downs. If a pleasure couldn't be immediate and mind-blowing, Yara didn't understand it. I pride myself on my powers of observation. However misguided I am as to my potency in this regard, I can assure you that I take myself seriously on this. My observations are always wrong, but I'm amusing to myself when all is done. The one thing I can count on is that I am always wrong when it comes to judging character, especially the characters of the people closest to me. I met Yara at one of the meetings of academic researchers in my field. What was my field?, you might well ask. I had flitted between Philosophy and Literary Studies, between Literary Studies and Political Thought, between Political Thought and Cultural Studies. I landed somewhere among these disciplines in Interdisciplinary Studies. Yara wasn't a researcher; she was writing a play where one of the characters was an academic. I don't even know why my colleagues and I let Yara into our meeting. I don't recall, now, how Yara came to find us in the third-floor Philosophy Lounge we had commandeered for our biweekly discussions. We, the academic researchers at the meeting, were flattered to a degree when we heard of Yara's plans, but preoccupied as we were with the urgency of our research we found Yara naive—yet mystifying, as researchers find art-ists. Artists seem to produce, by magic, moments of illumination. We academics, on the other hand, slog away at an idea, often only reproducing the ideas of others in our turgid and lethargic dissertations. So Yara's interest in us was amusing for some and alarming for others.

I was still considered a glowing presence in my department despite my foreboding that I would never finish my dissertation. It was now five years since I'd begun writing the work in earnest. I'd given many talks at MLA conferences, I had pub-lished five articles in refereed journals—one per year, which is a feat. Still I couldn't help but feel that my life's work was ebbing away in these grim halls we call academia. I had anticipated being done by now, but what with one thing and another, not the least of which were my personal entanglements, here I was at thirty-four with my dissertation incomplete. ABD. All but dissertation. In the academy, you get caught up in the cut and thrust of theoretical argument and theoretical doubt and before you know it a year has passed, and then another. I had been attacked by some colleagues who were jealous at my production. Naturally, these attacks were not open— but I had several theoretical knives in my back administered by the same people I was sitting with now. They sneered at the speed with which I produced papers, implying that my work was slipshod. I had failed to mention Guattari here, I had not cited Lacan there. One has no friends in academia. One has colleagues. One has assassins. I preferred my own company anyway. Or, to be candid, I was finding it difficult to cultivate friendships. Lezama and Jonesy had left the city and I realized that although I had thought that it was I who had been the glue of us, it was really Lezama—for various reasons, not the least being her bubbliness and Jonesy's desire. She had been the vivacious centre of our friendship. I think that desire is contagious.

There were five of us in the so-called study group: Josie Ligna, the deconstructionist; Abby Guarino, the Lacanian-feminist theorist; Ahmad Khan, the

Marxist theorist; Kofi Alexander, the Foucauldian theorist; and me. My work was interdisciplinary and uncategorizable.

Yara was a fresh gust of air that afternoon. I felt her breath rustle the dead paper dust that had settled on the rest of us in the room. Each of us, the academics, rose to the occasion. We tried to impress Yara with our gravitas. We were aware of her as one is aware of a lake of shining water along a path or a bright light from the sun through a window into a dull room. More the latter, Yara burnished the third-floor lounge. We overwhelmed Yara with multi-syllabic words and esoteric concepts, each of us thinking that we weren't really trying to impress Yara, we were merely speaking in the way that we, and people like us, spoke. Whether this worked on Yara, I don't know, as we were soon caught up, as usual, in the sounds of ourselves. Academics become anxious with their own self-doubt, and instead of this silencing us, the self-doubt only causes more logics of self-proving. So after a while, to us, Yara wasn't in the room at all. We insulted each other over who knew the literature of our subjects better. We pulled out little-known French theorists and quoted from them in French. One of us dredged up a Romanian who had written a single but seminal book, which the rest of us were unaware of. That stopped us for a milli-second before we collected ourselves, pointing out the flaw in the Romanian's unknown theories. We were amazing that afternoon as we whipped around like so many gleaming switchblades.

When I was a child, my grandfather had a way of feigning impatience with my questions while really being amused and fascinated with my argument. I had caught him smiling many times after dismiss-ing me. This is how I now dealt with my colleagues— as vague annoyances, though on this occasion I felt like slapping them all. Yara's delight and innocence— or what we then thought of as innocence—eventually brought us back to ourselves, or back to her world, or rather, the world outside of our research. This is what I loved about Yara—her pure delight and her sharp, if unscholarly, insights. Her shrewd observa-tions surprised me. Given the methods of my own scholarship, it would have taken five or so years to arrive at these insights myself and commit them to paper, and so her insights shook me and made me consider if there was not another, clearer way to look at the world. Perhaps knowledge could be arrived at from a more visceral and intuitive knowing of the world instead of the way in which I had so far been conducting my inquiries.

Needless to say, in my usual way I had misinterpreted Yara—or let us say, underestimated and badly assessed her fount of knowledge. But that is for later. When I first met her, I was very taken by the genuine delight she shone on all things. She giggled from time to time as we bore on with our academic minutiae. Her giggling at first goaded us on to more and more arcane hermeneutics until we finally subsided uncomfortably, each thinking we had made a complete ass of ourselves and perhaps created enemies amongst ourselves with the ferocity of our critiques. At the pregnant lull ending our discussions, Yara put us all at peace by declaring us fabulous and thanking us for including her in our meeting. She took each of our phone numbers, joking about how sexy she found us. Naturally we all fell for this and temporarily forgot all the theoretical wounds we had inflicted on each other in the course of the three-hour session. Yara complimented us, saying we were like wild and exotic animals she'd never encountered before. She said our brains were as sharp as needles. We'd never thought of ourselves as exotic and I for one was so taken by the metaphor I fell in love with Yara. I was willing to have Yara define the way I hoped to look at the world from then on. Yes, I *was* in fact exotic and sharp as needles. I'd never met a woman like Yara, a woman so forthright and brassy. Yara said what was on her mind all the time. She did not dissemble. She said she didn't know how to lie and that statements simply burst out of her no matter how uncomfortable. She said that when they came out she understood herself more. Why keep things inside, she said.

That afternoon, while we academics tried to collect and curate ourselves around Yara's descriptions of us, Yara shocked us all with a question. "So who do you people fuck?" she asked. No sooner had we thought her charming than we thought her disrespectful. We became defensive. One of us said, "Well, that is not a theoretical question." And another someone covered her mouth in dismay, and someone

else gave out a huff of disagreement. I smiled enig-
matically, and my closest academic rival, Josie Ligna,
gathered some words about theory and praxis, mock-
ing the academic who had denied the theoretical
implications of "fucking." In the end, our failure as
theorists was apparent, since if we were theorists of
the kind we'd hoped to be, Yara's question wouldn't
have floored us or caused so much obfuscation. Yara
made a joke again, saying, "You're probably none of
you getting any, eh?" We all laughed and left the subject there, as if we were joking too.

Yara had no filter. There was no public and private
divide, no secrets either. Much later, Yara said to me
that she'd had enough of secrets in her past. I was
afraid to find out too much about that past, yet I also
wanted to help Yara sort out the past so that she could
go forward with double her abandonment. Again, my
do-gooder personality got in the way of actual reality.
However, you can't blame me for compassion.

After the meeting, where I became intrigued by
Yara, I waited for her phone call, as did all the other
academics who had been in the room that afternoon. Yara had flattered and embarrassed us, and

as academics we couldn't wait for the opportunity at rebuttal. My vanity led me to believe that I'd be the one receiving Yara's phone call and that I would be the subject of her new play. I didn't live in the world of art and had no idea about Yara's work. Frankly, I didn't consider art to be work but something given by the gods. Despite my flirtation with literary criticism, and my reading of poetry to myself and others as solace, art qua art did not engage me deeply. I was aware of the commercialized versions of art— popular movies, television, and radio. Suffice it to say those were uninteresting to me. The world of artists, true artists like Yara, wasn't so much uninteresting to me as remote. I shared, of course, with my colleagues the disdain for and exaltation of such artists. I found them airy-fairy, to use a vulgarism—that is, they seem uninvolved in the material world. I much preferred past literary figures such as Naipaul or Walcott or Dickens or Shakespeare. I preferred my artists to be mythic—understood in hindsight, which is the way contemporary society embraces art, as a sort of relic. In this respect I'm not unusual. Art exists not in the present but in the past, like beauty, or like a holy icon whose significance is essential and infinite. Art and artists are a subject I'm familiar with only in a global and abstruse sense. Is this a dreadful admission in one who considered Literary Studies as an academic route? Not really.

Yara called as I predicted, a few days later. Truthfully, she had disappeared from my mind except as an occasional whiff of good feeling that I had carried with me since our meeting. Her giggle had stayed with me. Once or twice I remembered looking up from my own intense contribution that afternoon, and seeing her resist a laugh, her hand to her mouth and a sheepish look in her eyes. We had seemed to share a private joke and this made me certain she would call me. When she called, she said "Professor ——" in a false Italian accent. I'd insisted on a point on Gramsci's *Prison Notebooks* when my colleague Josie Ligna had cited her unknown Romanian. I knew it was Yara on the phone, naturally, and I laughed. Then she said, "Would you like to come and see my work?" in the same Italian accent. I jumped at the chance and we arranged that she would leave me a ticket at the door.

I'm not a professor, not yet. I'm simply trying to finish this dissertation. At that point, when I met Yara, most of my research money had been pissed away, though I can't beat myself up for that. I tell myself, I enjoyed it. I ate it, I drank it, I spent it on women. Fine. Some distraction always intervenes—if not intimate relationships then money or jealous professors who want to steal my ideas. I am determined to finish this year. Though I know I say that each year. There are other reasons for my failure to complete my work that I prefer not to go into here. My distractions seem more compelling than the dissertation. Why is it that the mind can be caught up so heavily in feeling? We have been taught that the mind is more systematic than the emotions, that the mind can be marshalled and feeling can be sublimated, but this, I swear, is false. Feeling is more compelling and insistent than what we call "ideas." Understandably, this is my own theory. No citation. Just self-diagnosis.

When I arrived at Yara's event, who should I meet there but three of the other academics, including Josie Ligna. Obviously, Yara was not discriminating. I had been at pains to say to my colleagues how disruptive Yara's presence had been to our discussions—and now there I was. Mind you, we'd all agreed, all except for Josie Ligna. My embarrassment was momentary. I was sure that I could explain my presence away through some academic ruse. Yara was a local informant, I would say. I sat at the back of the small theatre, which had a bar. I sat as close as I could to the door in case I felt like leaving, and also to get a better view of my colleagues. Josie Ligna, I observed, had found her way to the front, close to the stage. Ahmad Khan, the Marxist, tried waving me over to the other end of the bar, but I ignored him. Abby Guarino, the Lacanian feminist, was at a small table making notes in a tiny notebook. The place was poorly lit, so clearly she was faking it. I couldn't see the Foucauldian, Kofi Alexander, anywhere.

Yara's "work" included a monologue from Toni Cade Bambara's *Gorilla, My Love*, which was very affecting. Then Yara produced an acoustic guitar and began to sing. It was then that I truly fell in love with Yara. There was something about the way the single light of the improvised stage fell across her, something intimate and vulnerable that appeared in her face. Intimate and vulnerable, not weak. Worldly. She sang a song she had composed about a girl laughing or about wanting a girl to laugh or wondering if that girl was still laughing. It was about a girl Yara had known and lost touch with, and whom she had shared happy times with, but a girl who was a little crazy and lived a precarious life. Yara sat there, singing this song, but she had left the audience watching and had travelled toward the friend she was singing about. The way she sang the word "laughing" made me know that it was not about laughing at all. It was about the recovery of laughter. I saw a loneliness and a great capacity for empathy in Yara. When she finished the song the room was quiet. She sat still, then untangled her fingers from the guitar, took a deep breath and returned to us. She told a joke; I don't remember it. It was to cover the vulnerable space that had opened up in her. Then she introduced a bass player and a flautist, and they played for a while and then the show was over. I wanted to go to Yara, put my arm around her or give her a glass of water. I wanted to say to her, "Let us go home." But I didn't. I slipped out of the club and walked to my apartment.

It was raining—an odd tropical deluge for a northern city by a lake. What had I seen? Why hadn't I stayed? I saw Yara and the girl in the song fighting the world so that they could laugh, and I saw Yara lonely for that friend. I saw them both abandoned to the world. I made all this up as I walked home, and I determined that whatever it took, I would be in the world for Yara.

I didn't have Yara's phone number to call and tell her all this. A minor but telling obstacle. Now I fretted that Josie Ligna had probably stayed on and insinuated herself, with gushing congratulations, to Yara. Josie had a way with women. At any rate, I was happy (grateful) to hear Yara's chirpy voice on the phone the next morning, saying, "So, Professor, you didn't like my performance?"

"No, no, no," I gushed. "It was wonderful but I had to leave for another appointment." "Appointment?" Yara insinuated. "Well, I'd like such an appointment with you." I laughed. "About my play, I mean," Yara said. "I'd like to interview you."

"Sure," I said. I thought I could hear an interest in Yara's voice, an interest beyond a mere interview.

I said I could not imagine what kind of play I would feature in. Yara was a multidisciplinary artist, she told me. She didn't see herself as limited to one genre. She'd been trained in opera but had made the transition to what she called "less militaristic art." She said that she did miss some arias, like "Dido's Lament" and "Casta Diva," but she didn't miss the brutal competitiveness and the power plays of the opera world. I couldn't imagine Yara as an opera singer—not that I know opera singers. I saw Kathleen Battle in action once—at the Roy Thomson Hall, a solo recital—imperious and splendid. She ordered her pianist to get her a glass of water with only a glance in his direction. Yara, while potent, was not cruel—except when she was being cruelly honest.

I'd never lived in a world of honesty. So perhaps I took honesty for cruelty. My upbringing was to be quiet if there was nothing good to say. My upbringing was to have nothing to say in public, since this would either expose one's ignorance or give far too much away as to one's intentions. Yara went around saying everything in public—the mark of an artist, I suppose. She had no "private," as I've said before. At the lunchtime interview that followed our phone call, she launched an intrusive inquiry. Where was I born, how did I justify being an academic, who did I sleep with, did I ever question my left-wing politics, my gender assignment, my comfortable life while good people were starving, my obvious class allegiances, et cetera, et cetera. And did I intend to make a living off studying people as if they were bacteria? Wasn't I perpetuating a system of hierarchy? I engaged Yara lightly on the surface, seeming amused at her questions. Underneath I was steaming to be challenged in this way. In the end I felt as if all my ideas *were* indefensible. I knew full well my ideas were defensible, but put under the searching blowtorch of Yara's questions, I was at a loss. I was put out by the mere fact of being questioned. And so the legitimacy of these questions, questions I would have readily asked myself, annoyed me. I had until then observed the protocol of not asking or entertaining questions of a personal or political nature. Yara's every question was an indictment of my positions. My positions were public and correct, but to be asked about them was an affront. Yara laughed at the end of every question and her face had a smile all the way through her interview. This made me uneasy. I couldn't wait to get to the end of the encounter in order to never have to see Yara again. She even found fault with the way I spoke, calling it cute. I asked her what was cute about being able to enunciate words or possess a vocabulary? She said, "Oh no, nothing, it's just weird the way you talk." I was incensed. Only good manners and a distrust of my own uneasiness allowed me to bear the rest of our lunch.

When Yara called again I let the answering machine take the call. I listened to her message at least five times before calling back. She was sorry "if" she'd overstepped. She'd sensed my embarrassment but there was nothing to be embarrassed about, she simply wanted to get to know me deeply. Perhaps some of the questions had been intrusive, but she really admired me and what I'd accomplished despite the society we lived in. Did I detect a note of amusement? Still, I was pacified, though I didn't know what Yara was referring to when she mentioned what I had accomplished. Nothing, it seemed to me. I was working at a small community newspaper now, editing ads and trying to sell a few. I couldn't bear the manager, who had big capitalist dreams for the crappy little rag. I was barely hanging on and hoping my dissertation would bail me out. Sometimes I worked as a teaching assistant for some incompetent professor whose job I was better at. I was finished with all of my course work and my comps, and really should have been much further along. My father had warned me that Sociology, Political Science, anything in the humanities—these were nowhere degrees and that I should have done an MBA. But that is all water under the proverbial bridge. I find business and my father insufferable. He owns three used-and-new car dealerships around the city and suburbs. He buys wrecks, fixes them up, changes the speedometer and resells them to unsuspecting people. I know this doesn't make him the worst kind of capitalist, but it's what he's made of my brother, Wendell, that I detest. He's made Wendell into a toady. I'd done my under-graduate work in literature, and so had my brother. Wendell was two years ahead of me and had encour-aged me. But constant hammering from our father about how were we going to put food on the table with English degrees persuaded my brother to do a master's in business. I saw him fold up his soul and put it in the bottom of his shoe. I felt pity for him until the day he told me the same thing as my father— looking me in the face as if we had never looked each other in the face before with any sincerity. And so I left literature to analyze the social and familial systems that drove people toward self-betrayal and blind conformity. I miss my brother. On the occasions that we talk, I sometimes hear a small sound of what he used to be come from the back of his throat.

But I must get back to Yara. I was fascinated with Yara's frankness. I decided to subject myself to this unabashed honesty. I thought that there was something in it I had to learn. There must have been a layer of dishonesty in me that I wanted to cleanse. Yara took me to clubs I'd never been to in my life—clubs with painters, musicians, singers, actors, pool tables, smoke, installations, private sex rooms and sex viewing rooms. In some of these clubs we danced, and one night Yara spun me around on the dance floor until I fell down with dizziness. I loved Yara for this dizziness. The whole time I was with Yara I was dizzy.

I stayed out all night with her and her artist friends, coming home at four in the morning sometimes. I abandoned the study group. I had been accustomed to long cups of coffee with my colleagues after our sessions as we carried on the same esoteric arguments. No more. Truthfully I didn't know what Yara would do to the study group with her questions; I was afraid. So for the first months I abandoned my colleagues and my dissertation. Ours was what is commonly called a whirlwind romance. I lost weight answering Yara's probing questions about my life, my thoughts, and trying to be as honest and open in my own questioning of her life and thoughts. I experienced the world differently. I experienced the world at the level of the skin. Yara made me see that I'd spent enough time avoiding my true feeling. I felt flayed. Yet, energized. Yara would ask the most intimate questions of the most unlikely people. The bank manager she asked about her sex life—Was she getting any? Yara would ask. Taken aback, the bank manager scoffed and turned her back, but the next time we visited the bank together, I noticed Yara and the manager engaged in a giggly private conversation.

Yara's questions were, in the main, of a sexual nature and under other circumstances I would've said that she was fixated in adolescence, but given that I myself never asked these questions, I was persuaded that a repressed side of me was being challenged. Yara told me I was repressed. She said that the first time she saw me at that academic jerk-off she had felt sad for me (she is the one who called it an academic jerk-off); she had wanted to protect me, and she felt that she would do this for me. How odd that in a setting where I was at the height of my powers, Yara saw my vulnerability. That is, she saw me as vulnerable. I didn't know what to do with this admission at the time. It made me feel comforted, though I hadn't imagined it would. On the other hand, it disturbed me because it revealed what I lacked and what Yara, in far worse circumstances than I, possessed. I felt it was incongruous that Yara would say that, seeing me, she wanted to take care of me. But that is all in hindsight. Truthfully, at the time, through Yara's eyes I saw myself as possible and open. Yara seemed to experience life in the immediate, in the present. I lagged back, observing the experience of life. This, I assume now, is what Yara pitied me for. Was there a life I wasn't living, I asked her at first, a life only noticed in scars and pains? I hoped that I would have an impact on Yara with questions of this kind. She, it seemed, had grown up in a world of hurts and pains, so I asked her if it was only hurt and pain that defined a life. How do you recover from a wound? I asked her. To recover isn't to betray or forget, I said. It's to resist the definition of the wound as the whole incident. What about the defence mounted in the face of the wound? I asked. If we gave each other anything it was this argument. She laid out scars. I . . .

Let me rephrase. Yara would bring strays to her apartment over the railway tracks—by which I mean not cats, not dogs, not half-dying birds, but half-dying people. You see already my failure to be human in the description of people as "stray," but let me explain. There were always at least two other people in her apartment; one drinking water in the kitchen with the thirstiest appearance, another with bags in a corner, trying to sort things out, arranging and re-arranging the bags. These were bag ladies and women just discharged from the mental hospital, and women running across the country as far away as possible from Saskatoon or Port Alberni or St. John's, running as far away as they could get from all traumatic events. I was afraid of these women. Some of them were glazed-eyed and some so cleared-eyed their gaze hurt you. They either looked past you or deep into your soul. Some had a violence to them, a violence Yara rarely saw. Why did I see their violence while Yara saw their vulnerability? When I objected to them, Yara became distressed. Or she accused me of being comfortable and middle-class and therefore having blinders as to who these women really were. I think that was true, in the main. My blinders. I couldn't see, beneath the film of appearance, who these women were or had been, let alone who they would be. That is key, I suppose—to be able to see who someone might be. But if I was blind in one direction, Yara was blind in the other. She couldn't always see danger. She didn't see the violence, or the other universe these women had already departed into because of the violence they had suffered. She didn't see that their rescue was impossible. They were walking in another territory and not even her hand across the divide would lead them back to anything resembling where she stood. But I loved Yara's compassion, her scary compassion. Yara's compassion was sacrificial. Most of us stop at the perimeter of self-preservation, but not Yara. There was nothing between her and harm. She felt everything and she let everything in. To be with Yara was to hang on to an open nerve. There were constant emergencies. All of Yara's stray women lived emergencies—emergencies that Yara was willing to be dragged into as if their life were her life, as if their jangling cerebral cortex were hers. I couldn't always bear this presentness of hers. She would eye me accusingly, asking why I didn't feel the same. Her face then was all rawness, so open to the world it was astonishing. She was forever wanting me to do something about the world. I thought that I was doing something about the world by writing my dissertation. Language and thought— the world—would change after my dissertation, the whole field of gender would be revolutionized. But Yara couldn't see this, or didn't agree. I asked her: Didn't her own art work to save the world? her acting, her performances? Perhaps, she said, but it wasn't enough. She wrote me a letter about this once. She wrote me many letters, but this one said:

> Mostly I disagree with you on this self-fulfillment of your dissertation. People die all over the world, live hungry, freezing, thirsty, war-torn, and I want to be out on the streets and you want to be thinking. You want financial security. You give up life to universities, to this thesis to be read by whom, bought by whom? You still don't even know the meaning of the word oppression. You are satisfied with that, and I am disappointed in myself. I should be out more in the streets. Right here people die of crack, people are raped, and we do nothing. I am missing something by being with you, though now I can't live well if you are not in my life.

I am missing something by being with you. It hurts me to read this even now, years later. Yara was always on fire, burning, burning, burning. Her letters ripped my heart open. I never knew where to put them, they were so raw and truthful. I have them even now, and they still burn my heart.

Yara and I spent a furious six months falling in love. This falling in love consisted of intense arguments and sex. My colleagues didn't see me for these six months, and when I finally emerged again, after phone calls from my supervisor, no one seemed to recognize me. I'd lost a great deal of weight and I now smoked. This was all due to the intensity of my encounter with Yara. I had only answered the supervisor's call because Yara had gone away to a gig in San Francisco with a troupe of actors doing a Lynn Nottage play. I have never missed anyone so much in my life. We both felt, I think, as if something terrible was happening. The trip was only to be two weeks, but I felt such loss being without her it was as if an irreparable damage had been done. I had to get a hold of myself, so I went to the university. I recognized something like horror in my supervisor's eyes—well, perhaps consternation. He asked me about my health. Health? I asked. What do you mean, I feel wonderful. Auer, my supervisor, and I were not personally close so I found this question intrusive. Yara had sent me a postcard. It said, "Having a coffee (decaf) in a renaissance café in San Fran. How lucky to have you in my life. Take good care, love, Yara. To justice and equality." I had grown thin with my love for Yara. Loving Yara was making me thin. Every moment took on such a potency, a metabolic potency. My whole body seemed made, exclusively, of straining muscle. A colleague, the Lacanian whom I was not close to, passed me in the hallway and said, "Look at yourself." I did not look at myself. I had not looked at myself for six months of love. I'd only looked at Yara. And I didn't look at myself that day or else I would've seen the rope and beam of love I had become, the spare and lit banister of love I had become. I was brusque with my supervisor, promised him another chapter in a week or so, and went home to miss Yara more.

Now that I think of it, I suppose I thought Yara an antidote to academia.

It's August now and I am watching a blue moon. Yara would love this. It would be misleading not to speak of Yara's complete zest for living. Were it not for me, all our days would have been spent on the streets protesting and all our nights would have been spent singing and playing games. Yara loved games, especially poker. On any given night, her apartment would be full of actors and musicians and mad women playing poker. Yara was always moving among us, probing. She was the centre of attention, she cooked, she asked questions, she made jokes. One of her favourite puns was on the word "celibate." If someone said they were celibate, Yara would ask them who they were selling a bit to, or for how much. Yara knew the sex life of everyone and made this news public. She loved being the centre of attention in this way, and she could size up a person quickly. Her acting career benefited and suffered for this ability, since having sized up the person she couldn't help but declare her assessment. I, on the other hand, have poor judgment. I never know who people really are. I look over their faces and I'm at a loss. I look at some broad outline that I alone see and on that spurious basis I make a determination, usually wrong. It took me a long time to admit that I'm a poor judge of character. I didn't misjudge Josie Ligna, however. She had kept in touch with Yara, going to her demonstrations while I sat in the library working on my dissertation—over-confident, eight months into the relationship, of my limited (in hindsight) prowess.

I blame my grandfather for this overreaching on my part—this sense that the mental overwhelms the physical, and that I could, because of my stronger arguments, my philosophy, occupy an unassailable position with a lover. In fact, this is an arena where I'm completely incompetent. My grandfather staked much on the intellect, and he also succeeded in having many women besides my grandmother. He demonstrated, to me at least, how the intellect frees one from the immediate. Moreover, my grandmother seemed content to me; she turned a blind eye to my grandfather's infidelities. Infidel. Breaker of faith. Heretic. These observations I make of my grandparents are, I realize, equally spurious. They are based on knowledge gleaned from the times my brother and I were sent to stay with them every summer, and overhearing my father and mother talk about them. My mother complained about my grandfather, her father, often. My own father chuckled through these complaints. But the times my brother and I spent with our grandparents were indulgent and idyllic. Our grandparents seemed more expansive than our parents. Both my brother and I couldn't wait to be loaded on a plane each summer and banished to Fort Lauderdale, where our grandparents lived.

I was pious with Yara. If pious is absolute faithfulness, I was a defender of the faith. I was pious to the point of poor judgment. Isn't all faith poor judgment, though? I defended Yara's outbursts, her insults, her intemperateness—and she had many inappropriate moments with perfect strangers. She was always pulling someone down a peg or two, or going too far with someone, and when they criticized her she was offended and hurt. Then I would have to put on my armour and go out and break someone apart. I always said that she was right when she was wrong. Then, when I tried privately to tell her that she was in fact wrong, she would either assail me for my bourgeois analysis or she would look so crushed that I had to withdraw the criticism and assure her that I was the one who was wrong entirely. If I couldn't convince her, I would wake up to her absence, and a letter that began:

Dear ——, what I can say is I'm sorry and should life have been different, should I have been able to change the time, to clean myself, to will myself to be more I would have. Some things are like cancerous sores that don't heal, and only time can say what will pass. That is me wishing never to have been in a nightmare, needy. I take what I need. It is not a choice. I brave aloneness, hatred . . .

Then I would have to find Yara and hold her, while she forgave me and I forgave her. Invariably it was I who retreated. These events never caused Yara to pause the next time before flying off at the mouth. They did, however, effectively close the door on my critique.

Yara and I lived together only briefly. I moved into her railway apartment for several months. I didn't give up my own small place, however. There I would repair to my thesis, my books, my private life where I sat still or lay on the floor. I'm a solitary person in the main, and when I'm alone I think about how solitary and alone I am, and I think of how I love to be alone and solitary—but then I think how sometimes this aloneness and solitude needs to be performed among a multitude, because I wouldn't, for example, go out into the countryside and find a cabin and root around there loving its solitude. But I do love the quiet of my small apartment, and I love there the noise of my books, the din of all my thinking. I even loved the detestable neighbours. There is a big lumbering drunk man to one side, and to the other, a man who plays R. Kelley's "Nothing wrong with a little bump and grind" to wake up each morning. I can see the lumbering drunk right now: he is at the House of Lancaster with his face on the bar. The bump-and-grind guy I never see, I only smell his strong perfume as he passes by my doorway. Between these two neighbours, I am an angel.

I couldn't live in the same apartment with Yara for long; her busyness disquieted me. There were people coming and going all the time, plays being rehearsed, concerts being planned. At first I loved this, and gradually I was hauled into the arrangements for this or that event. Suddenly I was acting in Lonne Elder's *Ceremonies in Dark Old Men* and Adrienne Kennedy's *Sleep Deprivation Chamber*. Suddenly I was Yara's background singer at a concert. I could neither act nor sing, but in the thrall of Yara this fact didn't seem to matter. I felt the slightest twinge of discomfort within myself. I'm not delusional, but I was convinced by Yara's argument that expertise was a bourgeois plot to keep people away from pleasure and yoked to grunting labour. This made sense to me following Paul Lafargue's proposition that appeals to the moral nature of work are the hypocritical and corrupt ideas of the bourgeoisie in their attempt to chain the hell out of the working class. Writing in 1883, in his essay "The Right to Be Lazy," he said, "Our epoch has been called the century of work. It is in fact the century of pain, misery and corruption." Lafargue ended his essay in this beautiful way: "O Laziness, mother of the arts and noble virtues, be the balm of human anguish." Yara felt that everyone could act, sing, make music, make art and more than that everyone should do so to save themselves from the compulsive machine of capital. This I fully agreed with, then and now. Nevertheless, I told Yara that my way of defying and denouncing the bourgeoisie was to write my dissertation, which would expose their corruption and hypocrisy as much as Paul Lafargue's "The Right to Be Lazy" did. Lafargue, of course, was Marx's Cuban son-in-law, and as we all know Marx did not like him or his essay—but in this one matter I think that Karl was wrong, entirely. Yara loved me and she understood, if not my thesis or how it mattered, then my longing to complete it. I am reminded that Lafargue and Laura Marx, Karl's daughter, committed suicide together. He wrote, "I die with the supreme joy of knowing that at some future time, the cause to which I have been devoted will triumph. Long Live Communism."

After six or seven months with Yara, I stayed in my own apartment more often instead of going to her railway apartment. I didn't like the comings and goings at her place. I wanted us to be alone. Yara didn't like this much. She was suspicious of the private and she said that living, just she and I, would be living in a world discrete from others. She said this was capitulating to the normative, the "heteronormative" to be exact. I had no comeback for that. Yara's analyses were always surprising. And they were often spot-on. I had to admit that even though I didn't see us in some heteronormative performance, I couldn't define or describe what we *were* in, and neither could I offer an alternative reading.

I didn't want to be strictly alone with Yara, as in some doleful romance, but I also didn't want to spend my every waking hour among what my grandfather used to call those "crazows." I admit that this was a crude and backward analysis on my part. Guattari at La Borde Clinic would have been appalled. And so was I. After all Yara was practicing a group therapy for the dispossessed. But, Chaosmosis aside I felt more and more the pull to do my own work, and looked forward to the pleasure of leaving Yara's bustling house to simply lie down on the floor of my apartment among my paper. I mention my grandfather quite often, skipping over my father, because my grandfather was my great defender and confidant. He inspired me to be an intellectual and brushed aside my father's commercial concerns, saying that pecuniary ambitions spoke of a picayune mind. He loved this antique way of speaking. Why, when there was all the world to think about, should we only think of money? he said. Money was easy, he said, it only required cunning. And so my grandfather underwrote the antagonism between my father and me. These are sometimes the tensions that cultivate revolt in a family. I doubt that I will have children to follow up on that tradition, but perhaps my brother will and I will carry on this function with my nieces and nephews so that there will be more of me and my grandfather in the world and less of my father.

I don't know why Yara said that I was after security; perhaps she saw some vestige of my father in me. Yet I want to suggest that Yara saw peril as security. Perhaps we identify whatever situation we are born into as security regardless of its objective conditions. Yara's childhood wasn't the easiest. She was bounced around from aunt to cousin to mother, and back to aunt again. Her father was a flugelhorn player. He travelled the small dives across the country in a boozy mess for his entire life. Her mother was a pianist and self-destructive. Yara told me she couldn't wait to grow up and get the hell out of family. Engels would approve—this we can extrapolate from chapter two, part two, of *The Origin of the Family*. There was our similarity: I, too, couldn't wait to escape—in my case, the consumerist ambitions of my family. I can't blame Yara for trying to love newly. I too wanted to love in a new world. And for the time

we lasted, we tried every day to love this way—
sharply—making sure we weren't re-enacting the
heteronormative dramas of the ruling ideology. This
is, was, a difficult thing to do. There are no forms to
follow, only errors to make. The love was exhilarat-
ing but Yara's many projects were exhausting. I hope
it isn't the case that I was exhausted by loving. I hope
not. I hope not. I loved Yara, I swear. I didn't want her
to go. But if I'm a solitary soul, Yara is a gregarious
soul. She met many people and migrated into their
lives. She used to arrive at my apartment calling out
someone's first name as if I would know them. She
spoke of these people so familiarly, as if she'd known
them all their life. Toni, for example, where did Toni
come from? Toni had once been married to an eastern
European physicist who now worked as a mechanic
and who was looking for Toni in order to kill her.
Toni needed Yara's protection and a group of activ-
ists to confront the mechanic. Mechanics are by
nature a violent and disruptive force, as became
apparent to me later. But Yara attracted emergencies. She was like the fire department. I wanted peace.
The philosophical question for me became how to

reconcile the clear and dangerous everyday and dreadful emergencies of the social world, and one's obligation to rid the world of them, with the desire for peace, for calm in this social moment. You can see how it wouldn't turn out well for me. Again let me restate the philosophical question: how to avoid burning up in the incinerator of Yara's urgencies, that were my urgencies also, and still survive the cynicism of inaction. With Yara it felt as if each moment was crucial, and each moment stretched between these precise coordinates.

During this period my thesis did not go to complete shreds. Yara's energies led me to the following insight in my sixth chapter:

Certainly, Genet's The Blacks *concerns the confrontation between colonized and colonizer and speaks eloquently to the racial situation in the United States. But it is not primarily concerned with the experience of black people. Rather it uses their experience both as metaphor of more general aspects of the human predicament and as mask for Genet's personal experience and philosophy. In so doing it engages the traditional use of the stage figure of the black. Where the cultural ground is white, the black figure on stage is "figure" on a white ground simply because the ultimately stage reality is that of a white audience. Genet insisted that there be a white presence in the audience always, as the acts on stage never take place outside of the context of white dominance. Is it ever possible, in a white cultural context, to portray black characters on stage as other than metaphorical expressions of aspects of whiteness? One possible reply is that this figure will cease to exist when the political ground ceases to exist; when the black is de-metaphorized and the white made metaphorical. Genet himself said, "This play . . . is intended for a white audience but if it is ever performed for a black audience then a white person should be invited every evening. But what if no white person accepted? Then let white masks be distributed to the black spectators as they enter the theatre. And if the blacks refuse the masks them let a dummy be used."*[2]

Yara's flat near the railway tracks was a study in *précarité*. It was above a store in a strip mall. The strip mall seemed abandoned, the railway triangulating it, stranding it in desolation. Where I saw *précarité* some,

---

[2] Sanders/Teoria

Yara included, saw a crossroads, an opening, a choice. Robert Johnson, they say, made a deal with the devil at such a crossroads, which was why his music was so full of the divine, his gifts everlasting. There was a Chinese restaurant downstairs and a palm reader, Mrs. Carvalho's. Mrs. Carvalho gave discount readings to Yara's visitors, telling them what they already knew—that life was a bitch and beware the Plain of Mars. Here's the finger of Saturn, Yara would joke.

As intense as we were in our intellectual and sensual encounters, Yara was a jokester. Of course one aspect does not preclude the other; I'm talking as if sensuality cannot be humorous, or the intellectual fun. We found such pleasure in knowing each other's minds, each other's thoughts; took such pleasure from a surprising coincidence of having heard the same song at precisely the same age, or having been to the same club ten years before on the same night; or realizing that when Roberta Flack did a concert in Hamilton at the Coliseum we each quite separately, and in other lives at fourteen years old, took off from our homes and saw Roberta Flack together, without knowing each other at all. It was as if we knew each other before we met, and we simply had to slough off the unintelligibility of our former lives to arrive at Yara's flat over the tracks and meet again.

I loved Yara. I cannot say it enough times. I loved Yara as I loved myself. Or as I loved myself as another self, with Yara's coordinates. There will never be recrimination between Yara and me. I know this because Yara opened the terrain in me for feeling. I'm not saying that I was able to traverse the entire geography of that terrain, but I became aware of its existence. Because of this discovery, I can't in good conscience relitigate our time together in the common way of other people. I won't go over it and whine about the things that happened. I will not accuse Yara of betrayal or abandonment. I don't have hard feelings toward her. I have only gratitude for being jolted awake, by Yara, from the slumber, the disturbing slumber of the normative. Each day with Yara I was drenched in relief. Some days I felt as if I'd escaped from a prison camp—the prison camp of my former self. When you have escaped from a prison camp, all the leaves have a new tint, as do all the cars; you have a new skin, and all the people around you, you see with a new alertness. From Yara, with Yara, I entered the life I now have, like emigrating to a new country. But let's leave the similes there, since like became is.

What I did not know was that while I sat in Yara's kitchen and stared at the sink, sublimating the movement of Yara's friends around the room, while I caught a thought deeply related to my thesis topic, Josie Ligna was busy at work undermining my connection to Yara. I'd decided, under my new dispensation, that jealousy was a vestige of the heteronormative practices that I despised. So when I found myself in the fawning presence of Josie Ligna at Yara's flat, I observed her without erupting into verbal assault. I'd never seen this side of Josie Ligna. I'd only been privy to her knife-like intelligence, her murderous analysis and her forensic ability to dig up obscure Romanian theorists. I now wonder if Josie Ligna hadn't written those texts of the unknown Romanian herself and then presented them to us because we wouldn't have accepted them as her original ideas. Josie Ligna, I knew, had once lived in a threesome. She was far beyond my naïveté. The man in the ménage had been a dubious soldier in Srebrenica—a scorpion. He had tried to force his dreadful story on me once when our study group met at Josie Ligna's townhouse. I don't know what he saw in me that led him to the conclusion that his story would be safe with me, or forgiven by me. I was offended and, at the same time, terrified. There was an aura of threat about him, even as he begged for forgiveness. His body had a cat-like threat to it, ribbed but sinuous under the kurta he affected. So he stood there, at once prepared to purr supinely as well as pounce. This is the way power works—it wants both power and forgiveness. I hate this kind of greed in the powerful, the belief that their most heinous acts ought to be understood and forgiven. And if not, they will kill you. This man, Josie Ligna's husband, was like this. Josie Ligna's wife was a timid bird, who said very little as she flitted around Josie. Between Josie Ligna and this man, what a life the bird-wife must have had, between the viper and the scorpion. Yes, Josie Ligna was a viper, albeit dressed in ivy. After the visit to her townhouse, the next time I saw her at the university, I asked

Josie Ligna what in hell she was doing with that guy. She said he was looking for redemption and that he had seen the inside of his soul, unlike many of us. Well, I said, "I've seen it too and there's a solid murkiness there." Josie Ligna thinks that she can handle any situation. She's a humanist, whereas I am a . . . well, certainly not a humanist. Humanism is the graveyard of people like me.

Having got tired of the scorpion and the bird, it appeared, Josie Ligna was now snooping around my door. What could she offer Yara that I couldn't? Total agreement. Suicidal agreement. I was galvanized by this thought. I'd seen Josie Ligna manipulate the scorpion and the bird. I had to save Yara. I rose from my chair against the wall, and foregoing any intellectual cut and parry, I said to Josie Ligna, "Get the fuck out of here, now!" I don't usually subscribe to this type of language and neither did Josie Ligna, so she was as caught off-guard as I. She, the snake, looked at me and knew exactly what I meant. We understood each other perfectly. Not our usual idiom but . . . The other people in the kitchen making posters or placards, or whatever it was, for Yara's new project stopped what they were doing with surprise. Josie Ligna gave a nonchalant shrug, collected herself and headed for the door. Yara had an astonished smile on her face. She burst into laughter, and between gasps asked, "What the hell! Where are you coming from?" Yara spoke like her mother, like someone from another era. "Where am I coming from?!" I said. "She is a snake in the grass." At this point I couldn't help using the cliché. "And she has her eye on you but I got my eye on her." I had no idea where this language had come from but it seemed appropriate. Yara's mother, the piano player, had once come to visit and this is how she spoke. The idiom was direct yet metaphoric and it warned of a secret knowledge and wisdom. The mood in the kitchen became festive. I sensed an acknowledgement that I had joined the band of Yara's strays, and I went back to my thoughts—specifically, to working out if I should use Eric Foner's *Who Owns History?* in my second chapter. John Blassingame would also be relevant to my thesis' purposes in terms of the effects of plantation life on masculinity and femininity. Right. A theoretical point was clarified. Yara came to sit beside me,

pressing her body against mine. She was acknowl-
edging my expression of love for her in running
Josie Ligna out. But I would like to think it was more
too—as if I'd rescued her from the machinations of
Josie Ligna. As intrigued as Yara was by these
manoeuvrings, she knew that Ligna was a different
proposition from me. I loved when Yara sat next to
me like this. Also, sometimes when I was washing
the dishes and I was angry with her, she would come
and stand silently next to me, then reach to touch my
hand or my back. She would touch my hand or my
back, then lean against me, and all my anger would
dissipate. I would forget what I was upset about.

Josie Ligna was not the only person I had to drive
off from messing with Yara. Yara had many infatuations; people were drawn to her for the same reasons
I was. Yara encouraged these infatuations, and generally I did not see them as a threat. I sometimes
think that Yara brought these infatuations to meet
me so that I could get rid of them for her. She was
kind-hearted and could not do so herself. I have said,
I see the world from a cautious angle—even though
this view is never beneficial to me in ways I can

discern. I can see after other people's well-being but not my own. Accordingly, I could analyze Yara's loves and infatuations. I could tell which ones were trouble, and to a great extent Yara trusted me with this, since, as brave as she was, she was defenceless against perceived need. As I told her many times, not all need is need. Some people have bottomless need and it can swallow you up. Once, I remember, Yara brought someone all the way home from a trip abroad, from Tokyo, someone highly infatuated with her, and I had to take that someone to dinner and soothe her because Yara disappeared for two days. I didn't mind. This woman was lovely, the kind of woman with a sense of humour and esoteric information, like how to diagnose camber on an axle and how to use a wrench. Her name was Chiyoko and if we hadn't met under these circumstances we could've been friends. So we hung out for two days until Yara returned and found us putting in the new elbow joint under the sink. Then Yara threw a tantrum, saying she had a play to rehearse and could we leave? I drove Chiyoko to the airport and promised I'd get in touch if I were ever in Tokyo. Josie Ligna was another kettle of fish altogether. I note that I seem to fall back on verbal clichés only in reference to Josie Ligna. Perhaps only colloquial speech at its most reductive can express my outrage toward her. Or perhaps none of Josie's and my regular academic speech could express our desire for Yara.

Yara travelled a great deal, to Fringe Theatre festivals around the world, to international mobilizations for human rights, and to counter economic summits to the G7. I wouldn't say each trip, but often she would return with someone else, someone like me and unlike me, someone who had come apart in their life and ideas. Then they would meet Yara. And how could I blame them for their infatuation—after all, it had happened to me and I was grateful. I couldn't bind Yara to the normative, to an uncritical monogamy, a monogamy unexamined and taken for granted. And I couldn't deny Yara the full and true expression of her sexuality, especially on the basis of an uncritical acceptance of the norm. The normative was a doldrums we had all been lured into by the forces of capital, et cetera. This is what I knew and felt, even as I also felt a certain sting of jealousy and loss whenever one of these people showed up with Yara. In my analysis this "sting" was a vestigial emotion that probably predated capital, or perhaps had its root in capital, but was nevertheless what remained of different social relations and circumstances. My theory of myself is that any idea I can understand— that is, if it can be explained along ethical and moral lines as essentially unharmful, and as contributing to my intellectual life, my growth as a human being—I will embrace. And who was I, my theory theorized, who was I to claim hegemony over Yara's body? I've never wanted control of anyone, least of all their body. And least of all Yara's. Yara. I wanted Yara to have all she wanted.

The final woman Yara brought to her apartment tried to kill herself. She was from Sweden. The moment I saw Marit, I pulled Yara aside and said, "I'm not taking care of that one." Yara grinned in a nervous way, then became defensive and said, "I never asked you to take care of anyone." Then she laughed. But I saw her impending desperation. Yara had made a proposal to the Fringe Festival in Stockholm. Someone named Marit had heard of Yara's work and invited her to submit. Then this Marit had arranged everything and Yara was on her way. We had parted at Pearson airport in Toronto and she had promised to call me as soon as she landed at Stockholm Arlanda International. I was frantic when I didn't hear from her the next day, and then for a week. I read the newspapers; there were no plane crashes. I called the main Fringe line and received this message: Stoff, står för konstnärlig frihet, chansen att få pröva sin idé på en publik, möjligheten att skapa nätverk och kreativa samarbeten med andra artister samt att få utvecklas och inspireras från en uppsjö av konstformer.

I could make no sense of this. It was just advertising, I expect. I extrapolated creative from kreativa.

Finally, I searched Yara's desk for some contact she may have left behind and found a Marit Ahlstrom at the Blackeberg Station Theatre. I left a message with a man named Allvar and a week later Yara called. She said, "Hi . . ." then there was a pause. I said, "Why haven't you called? I've been worried!" She said, "Oh, everything's fine. Why would you worry? I'm here at Marit's." As if I should know! As if she'd told me this is where she'd be. At the someone called Marit's house! As if I ought not to have raised the alarm about her disappearance. I said, "Okay, see you when you get back!" and hung up. I knew that Yara was in love.

Yara returned three weeks later, saying that Marit would arrive in a few days. I went back to my apartment in a state of upset, having swallowed all my inclinations to cross-question her as to what was going on. After all, I knew what was going on—Yara was in love and Yara would soon be out of love and I would have to drive Marit to the airport and say Yara's goodbyes.

I saw right through Marit when I met her. She was not transparent; she was absent. I take that back. There was someone there, someone so concentrated around an incident, or a day, or an experience—and I struggle here to identify what, but some concentration so inevitable it was pinpoint small. And, I hesitate to say, lethal. I said to Yara, "Who is that?" And I said to Yara, "You have no capacity to fix her." Yara always dismissed my misgivings, and in the main she was correct about my trepidations. I'm not inclined to mix it up, to dirty my hands in other people's lives, and I am often wrong about character. But Marit was absent in a way that none of Yara's other projects had been. In my opinion, Yara herself often stepped over the line—her own line. She misjudged also. And with Marit, Yara and I came to an impasse. I was tired now of the constant upheaval of the physical and mental space of our relationship. I had my dissertation to worry about and I couldn't bear to watch Yara prance about, Marit in tow, repeating and espousing the same formulas about class and class war—Marit, silent and adoring. I stuck to my own apartment. I was conflicted, naturally. I didn't quite know the threat Marit represented. I can't say that I spoke two words to her, nor she to me. She wasn't malevolent, but some indeterminate bad feeling hung over her. She had a furtive eagerness. I'm making all these assumptions based on little evidence, simply her look, and a feeling. Or perhaps I'm fudging responses based on Marit's subsequent suicide attempt.

It's often the case that some women fill themselves with the self of the beloved. Marit struck me as this kind of woman: an absence in her, waiting for Yara to fill it in. The few times I saw Yara and Marit together, that furtive eagerness in Marit, that vacant place mirroring all of Yara's antics, disturbed me.

A day before Marit was to return to Stockholm, Yara found her hanging from the bathroom door, a belt around her neck. Yara called me from the hospital. I hurried there. Yara was devastated. I kept her company during the days the hospital kept Marit under observation. We argued about what to do with Marit. I wasn't very helpful on that. I found Marit's act violent. I said as much to Yara. Why had she done this, I argued, it was such a brutal act—an act either to get rid of herself or to bind herself to Yara. It was dreadful, I said. While all this may have been true, it wasn't what I should have said. Yara accused me of being harsh. I knew Yara was terrified at the burden Marit now represented, and no doubt Yara was in a different position than I was. The weight of Marit's life was now upon her. I didn't think that Yara deserved this and I made many clumsy attempts to say this to her, realizing that I could only hope that some of what I said had a creeping effect. I calculated that eventually it would. Yara called me callous, jealous and harsh, but I felt that I had to risk these assessments of my character in order to save her. I didn't want Yara's dear life to be sacrificed to the millstone of Marit. After all, they'd only known each other a short while. I told Yara that whatever had brought Marit to this had nothing to do with her. "This surpasses you," I said. "It predates you."

At last, Yara brought Marit home from the hospital and nursed her for several weeks. I couldn't bring myself to visit. I called each morning to see how things were going, and of course I slipped in my advice to get rid of Marit as soon as possible. Yara would hang up in the middle of my diatribes. One morning, knowing it was I calling, she answered, saying, "Got anything good to say today?" To which we both laughed. This is when I knew that she was out of the hellhole into which Marit had plunged her. Yara had a wonderful sense of humour and it had been buried for weeks during the debacle. Marit's brother, Allvar, came and finally took Marit home. But the whole incident caused my relationship with Yara to take a turn. It didn't deepen our bond. We didn't grow closer. I grew more impatient of Yara's projects—human and political—impatient and wary. Exhausted too. And Yara, with whatever she had ingested of Marit's distress, became more frantic, creating more and more social advocacy projects for the homeless women she brought home—drama groups, soup vans, et cetera—all without money. Let me explain. I applaud Yara, but she had a new project every day and I saw Marits appearing everywhere. Our relationship didn't so much end as fade out in this flurry. It faded out in arguments and in comments from her about my lack of real commitment, and from me about her tendency for hasty judgments. I felt Yara's anger at what she called my indifference. I flung back that she hadn't tried to understand my work. I had to complete my dissertation—these things, too, have effects, I told her. She was unconvinced.

We are still friends, Yara and I. And some years later, I'm still writing my dissertation. I can't but feel that she was right about me. The daily evidence bears it out. I inhabit a small room in the world. Outside

my door, the dreck piles up and I do nothing about
it but think.

Odalys

I keep the photograph of Odalys face down on the top bookshelf. I am afraid of her spirit, to be frank. Odalys believed in spirits. I'm not superstitious in the least. You might ask, then why don't I throw that photo away. It's a picture of Odalys and me jumping the broom at our wedding, and I keep it to look at myself in another time and incarnation. Odalys herself is also in another time and incarnation, and I wonder who she is now. I wonder who she was then. Then, when we appeared in the photo, I thought that I knew Odalys and Odalys thought that she knew me. The photograph is a record of this knowing. Knowing is so liminal. Even knowing one's self. As well, the photo is as a record of the misunderstanding and misrecognition that it now transports. One can look at it the way I have in those last sentences. But the photograph, when it was taken, was taken to record a happiness. Not the misunderstandings and the misrecognitions. As I said, in the photograph I knew Odalys, that is to say, there was the Odalys that I knew. No, I didn't know Odalys, the more I think about it. I was yet to understand Odalys. I was yet to meet her. We'd met and knew each other in the formal ways of meeting and knowing and having intentions, in the general ways accepted as normal. We'd appraised each other, in the provisional way that lovers do, by attaching great depth and significance to the provisional. How, after all, do you "know" anyone? You take in certain physical and emotional characteristics that you've aestheticized, ignoring the facts. You listen to what a lover has to say, taking in the erotic music of their sound, their timbre, while dismissing the lyrics. Consider: "I don't like eggs." You never hear this statement, truly. You hear the statement's quirky chirp, not its unreason-ableness, nor its true intentions that are a criticism of your own habits. Nor do you truly listen to other statements like "I want to go on a cruise to Norway"; "I hate reading fiction, I only read biographies of famous people"; "I hate theory, what is theory anyway." That is why I hate, to this day, music with words. The words are always dreadful. The chords, the movement from one note to the other, these are bearable to me and seductive, especially because they say nothing that we are supposed to know.

I look forward to you, Odalys. We will sit in a vine-yard drinking wine. I said this to myself when I was sitting in a vineyard with an older couple. This couple seemed happy and at the same time separate. I look forward to you, Odalys. We will sit in a vineyard drinking wine. Before I met Odalys, these were the thoughts I had about the someone I would meet who turned out to be Odalys.

I never wanted to get married. I never saw the need nor did I have the desire, if those are different concepts. I said to Odalys, Why do we have to get married? In your eyes, what does it legitimize? My feelings for you? Odalys took these questions as wounds and I, seeing the wounds, did not like inflicting them. I couldn't carry on a decent argument with Odalys. She always ended up spiritually wounded, she said. I tried another way. I explained to Odalys what it was to live in ideology; I summarized Althusser. Affirming Althusser, Odalys refused to admit to "believing" in ideology. I said it's not a belief; it's how you exist. Added to this, Odalys wanted the most distressing manifestation of a wedding. She wanted a particular dress, she wanted rings; she wanted a priest of some kind. She wanted flowers and music and food. She wanted a public declaration; she wanted the most conventional performance of a wedding. I knew that Odalys resented my not having descended to one knee to present her with a ring. I asked Odalys, Can't we imagine a different method by which to express whatever this is that we are doing? Admittedly I had no alternate scenario laid out—and this is the difficulty with progressive politics, the scenarios of the conventional are so deeply ingrained, so routine and systematic, so normal that it's impossible to imagine counter-scenarios, or rather the counter-scenario leans so heavily on the scenario as to be disturbingly undifferentiated. Isn't it possible, I asked, that we simply live together as autonomous individuals who share at times drink and food and sex without becoming a corporation? Without privileging our weaknesses, and frailty, as the economy of our living? At the same time, it's important to note that that philosopher, Althusser, killed his wife.

As with all the things I'm attracted to, Odalys frightened me. I think that it's love I feel, but it's fear.

I'm anxious about my dissertation, as usual. It feels as if it'll never be complete. I plunge into one idea and it sets off other ideas and I abandon the first idea. And all this happens before I can write the past idea down. But primarily I'm working with Gramsci's definition of "common sense," which he variously defined as "the public and manifest form of the national culture . . . a given social structure's 'popular science'; . . . the traditional popular conception of the world—which is unimaginatively called 'instinct' although it too is in fact a primitive and elementary historical acquisition." I'm interested in a complete overhaul of the way we live. Sometimes I sit at a café and watch a street go by and I'm struck by the smallness of the social world. Others have drawn this conclusion before, but still we're like a colony of ants chewing away at a patch of earth unaware of the whole universe around us. Sitting there I feel strangely apart. The data from the exosphere, the Milky Way, the signals from another hemisphere flood in, giving me an awareness that does not illuminate me so much as make me resentful of the people passing by clutching their bags of groceries, fighting their petty wars, occupying the slender earth without seeing. It strikes me, therefore, how inconsequential the quotidian is. I might say under different influences that the quotidian is in fact the important thing, the beautiful thing. But that's for another day. On the days when I observe the dreadful gluttony and smallness of this present reality, I can't ignore the cravenness, I just can't. On those days I observe the persistent futility of these daily activities. When I say I feel apart, it's not that I feel superior, as if I know something others don't. It's that I truly feel apart, as if I am an animal looking at another species.

Again, what do I know of other animals to speak this way? I mean I feel the singularity of consciousness and not of the body. The body is an inefficient encumbrance, or liability—or a thing whose liability is obvious. It is fussy and fragile and unaware of itself as useless and futile. When I said all this to Odalys, she accused me of pessimism or snobbishness. She referred me to some higher power she is pursuing at the moment.

I was not the best person in the world. Forgive me for that admission. It seems honest enough to say it, but that honesty is, in the end, weaning sympathy. This is how a sentence begins sometimes: *I was not the best person in the world*. And then the speaker goes on to malign the person who was unable to forgive them their failings. At any rate, thinking back I recognize that in regard to Odalys I wasn't the best person in the world and I expected her to forgive this flaw in me wholesale. Odalys was her real name. She had been through several names, she told me, as she found her way around this city. She was Marta, for a cleaning job in the financial district; Angela, for a front desk at a lawyer's office; and Ségolène, for an interior design company. When I met her she was Ségolène, but she told me her true name was Odalys and she had begun life in a small town outside of Cartagena. This is what first endeared me to Odalys—this change-ability and self-creation. I immediately thought of García Márquez' Aracataca. I sometimes think that for an academic I'm far too seducible by fictions and that is how I get involved with the wrong person. In the town where Odalys was born (and I forget the name of it now), there was one bus in and out every second Thursday of the month. Odalys said she loved that bus as a child and couldn't wait to get on it when she grew up—never to return to, yes, San Basilio. When she said this to me, Odalys had such a look on her face that my usual curiosity dried on my tongue. It was a subject I decided that I would let Odalys return to in her own time. Whenever she did, I was silent. This way I learned that in San Basilio, each afternoon at 2 p.m. Odalys heard the nasal chime of the lottery seller saying, This is your lucky hour! This is your lucky hour! "Es tu hora de suerte, es tu hora de suerte!" These two events—the bus every other Thursday, and the call of the lottery seller at

2 p.m.—Odalys said, wrenched her out of her child-hood. This was Odalys' power over me. The power to silence me. What could I say in the face of her child-hood? Mine had been uneventful by comparison. She said the call of the lottery seller was desultory and hopeless in the hot afternoons of those years. He himself seemed without luck. His clothing was dishevelled, his shoes laceless. After he sold what little he could in San Basilio, he disappeared in the late afternoon, dust seeming to envelop him at the perimeter of Odalys' depth of vision. If he were offer-ing something that he himself had enjoyed, Odalys said, she might have forgiven him. If he'd come wear-ing fine suits and rings, he could've been excused. Even if his disposition were hopeful inside his dishevellment, he would have made a better case. That he came morose and ill clad, and made no effort at joy, dismissed his entire proposal, causing Odalys' rancour toward him. There was no need to sell poor people more disappointment and grief. Even as a child, without the words to say so, Odalys cursed him and consigned him to hell. Yet the people of San Basilio would buy his tickets and live in impossibility

until the weekly draw brought them back again to their present lives.

When I met her, Odalys lived above the auto-body shop on Affinity Street in the south end—just before the highway out of the city, beyond which was the lake. Above the shop one heard from below the constant clanging and pounding and swear words in various languages—a mix of invective, aimed at car doors and engines, in Russian and Polish and Italian and Brazilian Portuguese. The smell of engine oil, the smell of burnt metal and soldering material, mixed with Odalys' cooking in what I was sure was a toxic ether. I said to Odalys that this was atrocious, that she should move before some heavy metals sedimented in her blood stream. Odalys always had a worse story for me in response to any problem I pointed out. She spoke of how people disappeared or of how insects disappeared from the world, of how frogs disappeared, and on and on. In response to my worries, she got Marat, the owner of the auto-body shop, to build a large plant box atop the building; this way, she told him, the greenery would compensate for the toxicity of the paint and solvents and the soldering. Odalys planted herbs and grapevines in this box, making a green canopy over the wrecks and carcasses of dismembered cars and trucks. When I stood at the bus stop across from Odalys' place on Affinity Street I recalled Adorno's statement, "There is no aesthetic refraction without something being refracted, no imagination without something imagined." I decided that I lacked the "imagined" that would imagine what Odalys imagined in that derelict place. And in my dissertation I was investigating that very imagination, the ability to see beyond the flatness of the existence that I attend to—my own. I couldn't imagine what Odalys imagined along Adorno's calculus. I only had Odalys' imagined world, her world as she imagined it and described it to me.

There had been nothing in San Basilio, Odalys said—nothing for her, at any rate. Odalys said she saw this as soon as she was born. Odalys claimed to have her first memory as a baby, in the arms of her mother. She said she remembered a stranger pinching her cheek, leaning into her face, and she remembers how upset she was at this. I asked her if she meant her mother. She said of course not, it was someone else, a man or a woman—she couldn't tell at the time, but someone strange. She thinks that she was only days old and it was when she first opened her eyes. This memory has followed Odalys. She always thinks that there is a strange, curious and intrusive being staring into her.

Now that I think of it, Odalys loved the auto-repair place because of the noise, the cursing, the clanging. A recipe, she said, a balm for the dead silence of most of her young days. She would pause at this, and drift far away from me. Her childhood seemed to me like a pause, a space in a room. Any room we lived in, my own or hers, the pause occupied like an object. Sometimes, when she did not know that I was looking, she stood in front of this pause with the look of a scolded child: her face turned down and away. That is the look I see in all our photographs. There is a pause where I should be. Odalys isn't looking at me, she is turned down and turned away from me. She is addressing whatever else is in the scene, whatever else . . . so I'm not there at all. I wonder at my lying in wait like that—that is the way I saw myself in relation to Odalys, lying in wait—coming between Odalys and silence.

These are all ramblings in the unexplainable. I have no idea what I'm saying and I never had any idea what I was saying when I was with Odalys. My academic life was irrelevant to her; it was like another kind of medicine that Odalys disagreed with. Why am I always finding women who haven't any interest in what I do? Although I must say, in Odalys' case my work wasn't so much uninteresting to her as it was unintelligible except as a source of occult power. Despite Odalys' hatred, her downright hatred, of her girlhood, she dealt in the arts of herbs and ridiculous potions and spells she had learned then. This is a big postmodern city and so you might not believe me—but the ancient arts of Africa, China and India and this continent are practiced beside the glass mountains of modern commerce. I learned this from Odalys. I'm not interested in the occult, and had I known how deeply immersed in it Odalys was, I would never have become involved with her. But there I was again, thinking that if offered a scientific analysis of the world, that is, a materialist analysis, anyone would jump at that rather than resort to magic. I'm delusional, as anyone can gather by now. I'm always trying to save women. But I remain confident that my intentions in the case of everyone I've mentioned so far were pure. Pure. As I said, given the materialist analysis that I was willing—compelled—to impart, you would think that anyone I was involved with would begin to gather a true sense of the world, not to resort to prayers, incantations and silences.

In the beginning it seemed that I was making headway with Odalys. She nodded her agreement when I analyzed the inequality sedimented in the relations of Third World to First World countries. She nodded, I assumed in agreement, when I said the Amazon was being eaten away by corporate predators. It didn't occur to me that my description of the Amazon probably sounded fatuous to Odalys' ears. Even when I launched into some more detailed arguments about the depletion of water because of soybean production, Odalys seemed to understand and agree. But then she suggested we recite a certain incantation each morning. Why in hell did she think that merely saying an incantation each morning would somehow dissuade these predators? How would they hear it? How would they know? I asked Odalys. How would they know that you are putting your magic arts toward the restoration of the Amazon and toward their demise? Come to think of it, they have their own incantations which are more powerful than yours. This kind of encounter, which increased as our time together lengthened, didn't strengthen our love. Odalys would withdraw, saying that if I knew so much why didn't I solve the crisis.

Can I say that I loved Odalys? I was more fascinated with than in love with Odalys, I suppose. I loved Odalys because she reminded me of a certain affect I experience at certain times or, shall I say, over the time of my life. That's not well put. You are born into time and place, more place than time, and the sounds, the colours, the gestures and movements of people around you come to form your aesthetic. I was in thrall to this aesthetic before I came to know Odalys. And so Odalys walked into my aesthetic practices. When I say practices, I mean the way I see, the way I apprehend pleasure, the sounds that are most pleasing to me, the touches, et cetera. Of course et cetera does me no good here, things must be listed, delineated. I loved Odalys' skin, pure and simple. I hate similes; they are usually so inadequate, I won't try to make one. Odalys' skin was ... Let me say from the outset I loved Odalys' body the way one loves a theory. Not, say, the theory of relativity—that would be too simple and unitary, I suggest. And besides, I know nothing of science. A theory such as the theory of language is more the theory that comes to mind. How it is acquired and why certain sounds occur in certain regions; the uses of the tongue, et cetera. A theory such as one suggested by Chomsky's works might best describe my fascination. To be more precise, it wasn't Odalys' body but the *sense* of Odalys' body, like a universal weight in the world. Perhaps, perhaps it was the weight of her presence, the "mental grammar." Sometimes I think I created Odalys out of what I needed, and what I needed was a balancing weight to my theories—some presence that would deny or counter those theories through embodiment.

To clarify, I loved Odalys' aura—the very thing I proceeded to try to get rid of in her. Or perhaps I wanted to understand it, to get it under my finger like an insect—to examine it. And when I examined it, there was nothing there. This is the disagreement between me, as an academic, and the world. And by the world, I mean my lovers. My lovers never change. It is as if I've loved the same person all those years. My lovers have come in different manifestations but they are essentially the same person. I don't know why I've redirected my account of Odalys in this way. Perhaps it's because Odalys filled me with a certain fear—so much so that I fear that giving an account of her life will violate her privacy. Yet I'm not certain of the truthfulness of what Odalys said to me about her life. And truly, when I think about it, no one owes me a proper and truthful account of their life. And I don't owe anyone veracity when it comes to mine. Odalys' life became more and more obscured, more and more hermetic to me.

I still have to figure out why I became involved with Odalys. Odalys was unconnected to any other part of my life. She was my experiment in the utterly strange. I tried to immerse myself in her life and the life of her friends whom I met, but here again I found myself at my peculiar angle. They belonged to a small community of Colombians living in the city. I barely understood Spanish and so their conversations were incomprehensible to me. But Odalys explained they were all from San Basilio too. They all, like Odalys, had a certain morose joy. I would feel my way through their conversations, thinking that they were speaking of some bad event that had occurred, and then they would burst out laughing. My angle toward them was patronizing, I have to admit. I therefore did not remember their names or their faces. In my defence, when most of your time is spent with pages, with the pages of a thesis, personal engagement can only be superficial.

I had never married anyone before Odalys. I became swept up in her machinations. I still don't know how. One day she asked me to marry her and the next day I was in a drum ceremony saying vows after a quickly arranged matter at city hall before a justice of the peace. Perhaps that's an exaggeration, perhaps it took two weeks or so, perhaps one month. There were rings to be bought and clothing to be decided on, so it must have been a month. At any rate,

the party was spectacular. Odalys invented the ritu-
als. I took part. I must've been at my most hopeless
when this happened, since I can't say that I made a
single decision. I had a view of myself throughout the
ceremony as someone looking in on a bizarre life.
I was the only person I knew at the wedding except
Odalys. Was I embarrassed? Why did I not invite my
brother? my father? my mother? Some part of me felt
self-betrayal at giving in to convention. But then,
I had drifted so far away from convention that I could
afford to participate in it as a curious and distant
exercise—like a researcher in a lost culture. I would
not have wanted my family to misinterpret this
experiment as real life, therefore playing into their
idea of normalcy. In any case, it did not matter; I was
not in touch with my family anymore. At certain
points during the wedding party, Odalys' friends,
laughing and dancing, sang the lottery man's nasal
song, "Es tu hora de suerte! Es tu hora de suerte!"
Odalys joined in and they danced around in a mad
embracing circle and fell down like children.

    I'll tell you how I met Odalys. I was walking along
a street where I had heard there was a bicycle shop

that sold good bikes for little money. I was given to understand that these were high-end stolen bikes— Nishiki, Schwinn, Colnago, Kalkhoff. I had decided that I should get a bike instead of using public transport. I can't ride a bike, but I thought buying one would give me the inspiration to learn and to save the planet at the same time, and also to save myself some money so that I could re-enrol in my PhD program in order to get a date set for my defence. I had deregistered to save money. I'm digressing as usual when it comes to Odalys. At any rate, I was in search of this store where Josie Ligna had bought herself a Schwinn when I met Odalys. She seemed to be retreating out of a nearby store when I wandered into her. My hands reached out to protect myself and she spun around and grabbed them. She said, "You're very cold. How come?" Her words were intimate, as if she knew me already. "I don't know," I said. "Let me warm them," she said and proceeded to rub my hands in her palms. It was July. She kept walking backwards, warming my hands. After several yards I tried pulling my hands away, thanking her. Her back was still in the direction we were heading. She said, "You're wasting all your light." I stopped. And she did too, looking into my eyes with the most knowing expression. "True," I heard myself confirming. I can't fully describe the comfort I felt in her words, in the realization that someone finally understood me. I felt as if I'd been waiting for someone to say this to me. *You are wasting all your light.* I hadn't had the words and here this perfect stranger had said them. It is true, I was wasting all my light on this insufferable institution that was the university—academia— and my cretinous colleagues, and the trolls of the ruling class who were my professors. It had become increasingly impossible to express a single original idea without these Neanderthals wanting you to weight it down like a sycophant with all the drivel that had come before. And here was this vision of my future, Odalys, although I didn't yet know her name, telling me, "You're wasting all your light."

Anyone could see how I would be drawn to her. Odalys held my hands and kept walking backwards, pulling me along. It was some time before I realized that she was walking backwards. We arrived at a traffic light, not noticing. Caught up in our fantastic absorption, I only became aware of people shouting as we almost stepped off the curb of the road in front of an angry white car. I pulled Odalys to the sidewalk, but she kept going in this backwards fashion and the noises subsided. I asked her why she was walking like that. She said, "Going home." I said, "I mean backwards." Odalys said, "I am trying to change life around. I want to see what was behind me before, I want to see what I leave behind when I move forward." Can anyone, any social theorist, deny the investigative power of this? the profoundness this involved? Wouldn't Habermas find this compelling? I would go even further. I would say that Césaire in *Discourse on Colonialism* would firmly fall in with Odalys' line of inquiry. And most recently, Gikandi and his *Slavery and the Culture of Taste* Odalys foreshadows here. Ordinary people have an acute grasp of what we are living—far more acute than we academics give them credit for. There I am, ending in a preposition. I hate doing that but it can't be helped. I decided to walk with Odalys and tell her about my life. I would face forward unaware of what I was leaving behind, and she would face backward, fully conscious of another realm of understanding and reason. Odalys and I therefore connected on this level, which I hesitate to call spiritual, since I don't believe in that kind of thing and I clearly overestimated how deeply Odalys was submerged in its efficacy.

Now in hindsight, I mistook Odalys' occult interest in me for affection. I'm always mistaking people. Her interest in me was like the interest of a doctor in a disease. She diagnosed my hands, my face, the look in my eyes, for symptoms from her spirit world. Some being, according to Odalys, was registering communications through me. That's what I gathered later from Odalys. My cough was a sign from somewhere about something. If I dropped a cup, some spirit wanted the water in it; if I spilled wine, I had failed to libate the ancestors; if an object couldn't be found, or appeared somewhere other than the place where I put it, it wasn't simply forgetfulness but the metaphysical manipulations of the people who had lived and died in my apartment before. I went along, blissfully ignoring the life Odalys was living, ignoring where she had located me in it, brushing away her baths in green leaves for money, her evaporated milk and anise baths for purity, her blue baths of food colouring and lavender and scrubbing shells with watermelon incense for peace, her red baths with beets and John the Conqueror herbs for courage; her purple baths, which she persuaded me to take with her, for power—and with these baths, the five-finger grass she made me put on my eyelids. All this I did for Odalys. I humoured her. Well, there's my paternalism again. I've spent my whole life suffering from this trait. People are always living a life I fail to apprehend. It's right in front of me but I go about with my own assumptions, drawing faulty conclusions that end up being fatal for me.

Odalys' place above the garage was full of the paraphernalia of her practices. That's why I couldn't live there even after we were married. Central to the main room was an altar. The wax of many candles crusted the floor; the masks of many ancestor gods peopled the walls. Always there was the scent of some uncertain burning and the sound of running water. There was a peace at Odalys' place; to be sure she was centred in her being. That last sounds like something she would say, *centred in her being*. Anyway it was true. I can say that Odalys had no anxieties—or at least, none I recognized. I was someone who lived in anxiety. I felt anxiety was a necessary part of being conscious in the world; it was a prerequisite of a moral and ethical life. I don't mean the anxieties of Capital, I mean the anxieties of an unfinished world, the unfinished project of the imagination, as Wilson Harris would put it. But perhaps here again I fail to recognize: Odalys' anxiety must have been to satisfy the anxieties of all her ancestor gods. They took all day long to appease—or at least, what Odalys did looked to me like an appeasement. No sooner was one satisfied than Odalys would move to another. My presence seemed to alarm them, and that is another reason why even after Odalys married me, we didn't live together. I visited Odalys above the garage each week; once every six or seven days seemed sufficient for both of us to be in each other's presence, so intense were our meetings, so cluttered by my thoughts and by Odalys' thoughts, which were unfathomable to me.

Of all people, Odalys understood my dissertation least and most. In many ways we were navigating the same territory. For what was it really but the explanation of how it is to live, and to analyze the forces arrayed against that living? How can I blame Odalys for trying to find a way through, albeit with magic? How can I now blame her when obviously my methods hadn't yielded any success? I suppose you can say that we were exploring different paths. I didn't anticipate any result from this, like peace or harmony or any of the claptrap Odalys anticipated. Nor did I consciously expect the disintegration of oppressive structures after my own dissertation was complete, though deep in my heart I did; but at the level of the intellectual, the cynical, I did expect to silence my colleagues and to move from sessional teaching to something more permanent. Your expectations get very small after watching the world awhile. Believe me. I also expected to find a publisher for my treatise, and then to shock people into finally listening to me. Now you might say that Odalys' ambitions were greater than mine, theoretically far greater, since she at least was trying to elaborate a theory of being while I was merely anticipating work and a publisher. But these thoughts are useless, since I

can't seem to find a way back to my dissertation.
I've taken to being maudlin. Yes, my work was important, and of course it will be groundbreaking. To
compare it to some senseless metaphysical maunder
isn't worthy of me.

By the time I met Odalys I can't say that I was still
in the best of moods about my dissertation. I was
thirty-seven. To tell the truth, my own apartment
was not dissimilar from hers except in one respect.
There were no longer any gods at mine. If I had
gods, they lay dead in heaps of primary reference
texts. There was no altar except the altar of my
depression. I would arrive home from Odalys' and
find the bitter piles of paper and books that littered
the floors and tables. They seemed to address me
with a kind of spite. It was not for want of writing
that the dissertation hadn't come together. I had
discarded many versions of the original thesis. My
filing system had begun well enough, nine or ten
years ago. I'd started with the greatest enthusiasm,
done my comprehensives, done my course work,
gathered my committee. I had been in the spring
of my intellect then, when I was twenty-eight.

Mathematicians have an early expiry date, they have a short shelf life, but philosophers only grow better. Clarity, with us, increases. Memory isn't the optimum quality, neither are pretty, young, green synapses. I console myself saying this now, but back then I felt I was on the brink of a great philosophical discovery. I had constructed my thesis committee in the hope that they would leave me be. After all, what could these antiquated senators of the dying regime possibly give to me? Their lives had been lived in privilege and elitism. They had fooled themselves into thinking that merely because they had privilege, they had earned it. They'd never taken into account the violence their existence had perpetrated on the world, on the very people who lived around them. They'd oiled their way into schools and clubs and journals and conferences. They actually believed that this made them worthy—they confused their privilege with intellect. These professors weren't conservatives, by any means. Oh no, they would never consider themselves in that category. They were left-wing scholars, social theorists. But I knew, and they knew, that academia was a place for perpetuating class and class privilege. It was a place for training up the ruling classes so they could continue ruling. My aim at the time was to write the bomb of a thesis that would blow up the buildings. Little did I fully recognize that the old farts on my committee would bog me down with their criticism about the structure of the thesis, the citations and proofs that were necessary, the "theoretical framework" and on and on with each iteration of the thesis I would give to them. No one can accuse me of self-indulgence. Self-criticism has been my practice since I was four or five years old—as far back as kindergarten when I borrowed a pencil from a rich boy only to lose it on the playground and have the teacher scold me for doing so. As young as I was, that teacher's tone told me just where I stood. When I came home and told my father, my bougie father, he shook me and scolded me never to find myself in that position. I never played with that boy again and I kept my distance from that teacher forever.

But to return to my thesis: it lay on the floor and tables and open desk drawers of my apartment, its theories scattered and shredded. The Chair had died after six years on my committee, and the second reader had left for another university. Josie Ligna laughed and said I'd taken so long that my Chair, like my ideas, had expired. I won't forgive her this zeugma at my expense. Despite finishing her thesis before me, she hadn't published half of what I'd published in refereed journals in our field. My apartment was desultory with unfinished chapters. I'd torn up at least three versions of the thesis, and these lay in the bottom of my kitchen drawer with the spoons and scotch tape. I'd torn them up but changed my mind and resolved to stick them back together when I had the time. Each evening I would look at these three versions and a paragraph would leap out at me: *I am especially interested in how unknown and/or unacknowledged histories nonetheless continue to produce symptoms; in how we reproduce the unknown trauma or desire that complicates and structures our lives; in how these unrepresentable or represented social structures or relations erupt in concrete ways in other times and other places. . . . What bodies, languages and ideologies are more or less readily included in constructions of communities? What memories are performed*

*and reformed in the border spaces of these texts? What
do memories entail, what do they permit and what do
they exclude and prohibit?* [3]

I would return to these words time and time
again. I'd written them in the earliest iteration of
the thesis and they still sounded utterly masterful
to me. Yet my deceased supervisor had pretended
not to understand this paragraph. I always called
him Professor Auer, despite his insistence that I
refer to him by his first name, Bertolt. I liked Bertolt
Brecht too much to call this doorstopper by Brecht's
first name. Let me be truthful, Auer never knew
that I hated him. He never knew, until the last, that
I dissembled at our every meeting. The levels of dis-
sembling that I'd been taught in my arriviste family
and among the people I was born to were completely outside of anything Auer could imagine.
Leaving his office, I would run to the elevator or
down the emergency staircase to prevent myself
from exploding. Or to prevent him from witnessing
my explosions.

---

[3] C. Sharpe/Teoria

My father had taught me well. "Don't let these people know that you're upset or see you upset. You're better than that," he would warn. "You're better than them." It was the only advice he gave me that I would take. And so I would never let anyone on my committee see me distressed. I would never ask for anything I didn't deserve by right. I reserved my true feeling for my theoretical work. Auer tried often to engage me, but I surmised this was only to give himself the occasion to belittle me. Often, when I was in his presence as he held forth on hermeneutics and Habermas, I thought to myself, "You have no idea, Bertolt Auer, how much my people have been through, and how it has prepared me for sitting here and listening to your bullshit without a word in response. You do not know." Each chapter I would give to Auer, he would turn over on his desk without looking and continue where he had left off the time before. After a month or so of waiting for his response to the chapter, I would hear that he still thought there were problems with the theoretical framework and he would suggest revisions that necessitated quoting his own work on the "public sphere" and "communicative action." Auer's theory was predicated on a "homogenous" that social structuring patently denied. He posited a simplistic analysis and failed to analyze the deeper underpinnings, economic and racial, of a far more complicated set of relations and locations. The histories, the violences he ignored were mind-boggling. I found his work essentially tiny and solipsistic; his ego, however, was massive. On several occasions I attempted to replace him as my supervisor, and this caused major eruptions of bad-mindedness on his part—and as if I were not having enough trouble writing the thesis itself, it delayed my work even further. No one wanted to cross him in the department.

Auer's death did not move me. Here I failed as a human being. When I heard of his passing I remembered Diane Wakoski's poem "Dancing on the Grave of a Son of a Bitch." That poem, at least, had previous affections it mourned. Not so, my relationship with Auer. My failure here, I freely admit. Death should move us. Auer deserved contempt perhaps, but not death. Yet I can't help but think that his rancid, life-sucking ideas contributed to his demise. Here again

I'm not being kind. I must confess, without embarrassment, that I felt somewhat renewed by his death. I would find another supervisor, I would finish the thesis and launch myself among the real scholars who would truly be my interlocutors and colleagues. This is what I'd hoped.

Bertolt Auer's death gave me a freedom. I felt my rooms open up. For a shining few months, my thesis seemed alive and possible again. And in the beginning that was true. I wrote copiously. A new idea came to me: I would write the whole thesis before I struck my new committee. I would overwhelm them before they had a chance to give any advice. The result of all this—the detritus of it—is gathered on the floor of my apartment. I never invite anyone over.

Odalys refused to visit me after a while, since when she did visit, she would try to clean the place and we would end up in awful fights. Her rearrangements would leave me with days of reassembling to do and set me back on my thinking. Once she tried to turn the oven on and almost cost me notes to several chapters. I know where every bit of paper, every idea, is located, I told Odalys, and I don't need anyone coming in here and disrupting things. *Both texts revise mono-narratives of the flesh by relocating memory outside the body rather than insistently stigmatizing the body through the reproduction of particular historical moments. Both texts suggest that it has become necessary to locate social memory outside the body.*[4] I love my apartment. It contains all the beautiful pages I've written, and all of my generative anxieties. I will admit that sometimes when I open the door I'm overwhelmed by my work. And I will admit that it prevented me from leaving, from going out to visit Odalys. These two ideas can exist together, I've now come to understand. When I went to Odalys', it was often with relief. I was happy to be away from my apartment, away from the unfinished business of my thesis. My life's work, I call it, and I suppose it's come to be just that, the work that will take me a lifetime to complete. Odalys' place couldn't have been further away ideologically from my rooms full of imprecisions, proofs, theories. Though I suppose belief such as Odalys' is theory of a kind. Odalys dealt in the

---

[4] C. Sharpe/Teoria

natural arts, I in the arts of . . . of what? My art is nothing, since everything is built on, or rather stopped, as a post stops a wall—built and stopped on someone else's suppositions.

"Teoria . . ." that is what Odalys called me. "Teoria, you are too much in your head. Before you can do something you think it out of existence. You think it out of being something to do." This was her reason for calling me Teoria, Theory. I can't fault her argument. But as lovingly as she said this, I sensed an insult and snapped at her, "Belief is a theory, isn't it?" God exists: thesis; Odalys is central to this existence: exegesis. But I could be entirely wrong about what Odalys thinks, since all her beliefs are shrouded in mystery. I asked her why her gods were so domestic, so small as to be concerned even remotely with her; she sucked her teeth at me. She told me, "You lack an anchor; you lack a thing that you love." I said, "But Odalys, I love you." She said, "Yes, you love me more or less, but I am talking about a love without limits, without reservations, without a face or a body." I was brought up short by Odalys, as I am sometimes by the most common charlatan selling god on a corner.

Their faith is to me so dreadful and overblown, there are no answers to them.

As I said, I think that Odalys married me as an experiment. She married me to see if she could convert me. She wanted me to be her acolyte, her cheval. She married me as a test of her faith. Her Babalao, who officiated at our wedding, was not impressed by my skeptical looks and told Odalys that while he couldn't prevent her from her path, our union would be full of difficulty. I knew that Odalys was smarter than this Babalao. She considered herself Iyalaoo, anyway—mother of divinations. Now I believe that I was one of Odalys' Nkisis: her Nkisi of academic theories. Around her apartment above the garage stood several fierce wooden figures, with nails and blades buried in their bodies. They signified power. The spirits could be released from, or contained in, these figures at Odalys' will. I can't help but think that I had a place among these figures and was at the will of Odalys. Though, as with these spirits, Odalys didn't always have full control.

I don't know how I came to leave Odalys. It is one mystery too many, I suppose. But no, in truth it is

Odalys who left me. One night I noticed a certain odour on Odalys' sheets. I couldn't immediately quantify it, since the garage below Odalys' apartment had infected the floorboards above with many smells. This was an odour Odalys never noticed but I had trouble getting used to. I couldn't offer my own apartment for our sleeping, since all of it by now was taken over by paper, even the walls. And in any case, Odalys felt she was in harm's way without the presence of her Nkisis guarding her palace. I remarked on this new odour to Odalys, and she said I was always finding fault. I lay back under the sheets and watched Odalys fall asleep unbothered. The odour—of soldering metals mixed with an unknown substance— seemed to envelop the bedroom. The next evening, on my arrival, I noticed a new Nkisi standing in one of the shadows of Odalys' rooms. It struck me immediately as more aggressive that the rest, and there was a sly look to it; a thorough covering of nails and shanks adorned its body. It seemed prepared to fling them all at me. I said to Odalys, "That's new"—pointing to the Nkisi. "It's been there all the time," Odalys answered. She said this with sarcasm, as if I never noticed anything about her. I kept quiet but I felt as though another person were in the room with us. And again, there was the strange odour of the sheets. After two more nights of these aggressions, "Odalys," I said. "What's going on?"

"Marat was here earlier."

"Marat?" I said, "Who is Marat? Marat!"

"You know Marat," Odalys said, indignant. "Marat from downstairs." Marat, the mechanic! The alliteration made me ever more angry.

"A mechanic, the mechanic!" I sputtered at Odalys. Odalys shrugged, and the nail-prickled Nkisi stood closer. I had once made a joke about this man Marat, with his perpetual wrench and his dirty hands— something about the Marquis de Sade, his namesake.

"Well, who's the bourgeois now?" Odalys said.

I rose to leave the room and the Nkisi stood in my way.

"You're leaving, then?" Odalys said.

"Yes," I said meekly. There was a pause and then the Nkisi seemed to move as if on Odalys' command. I took my things, my bag with the chapter I'd re-written at the library, and left. I never went back to

Affinity Street. I didn't want to see what Odalys was doing with the mechanic. She didn't call and I didn't expect her to come to my Augean apartment, ever. A mechanic. Odalys preferred a mechanic to an intellectual. I could see the practicality in it. After all, what can I fix? Not a damn thing. My angle on the world didn't see Marat. I am vain in reference to myself, too vain to see what is in front of me. All this time, I'd been focused on arguing with Odalys' metaphysical world—and her material world escaped me. I saw Marat but I didn't calculate him. I didn't place him in my equation. He was, to me, mere atmosphere. And yes, I have to reconcile myself to Odalys' accusation that I am bourgeois. I was not. I wasn't, I protest, so insulted by Marat's status as a mechanic. I admit mechanics do a lot in the world. My outburst was without legitimate foundation, and all I have to say in my defence here is . . . okay, I realize immediately that what I have to say is bogus. Nevertheless, Odalys, what about my light? That's what I will say to her if I ever see her again. What about my light?

My outburst was a coarse and illegitimate refutation of all I stand for, all I care about. It caused me pain. What happens when we reproduce the backward ideas we abhor? When they spill from us like so much bilgy sediment? I retreated to my apartment to think about this. Not even Gramsci could save me. A mechanic! I hear the outburst ringing in my ears to this day. It seems the "anachronistic" and "fossilized" conceptions of the world were all too evident in my being. Knowing better hadn't prevented that concept from leaking into my own life. One course would be to apologize to the mechanic, if not to Odalys. Odalys didn't deserve an apology, but Marat, despite not having a clue about my judgments—and perhaps because he had no clue—deserved my apology. I decided that if I felt bound to do anything, it would be that. This secondary pain, the pain of my personal betrayal of my ideas, was excruciating to me. And it stood in for the pain of Odalys.

I had discovered Odalys' infidelity through the odour of soldering metals. I put it in those words so that I could give the whole episode a poetry. Once I did this, I felt no rage against Odalys. But isn't poetry one of those anachronistic and fossilized conceptions of the world and life? Or isn't poetry the conduit through which anachronistic and fossilized conceptions of the world and life are transmitted? Possibly, but it will do, I told myself, as a way of positioning Odalys and me for the time being. For months before our denouement Odalys had been encouraging me to concentrate more fully on my dissertation, suggesting I stay at my place and bring it to a conclusion. I had never suspected a thing. I took her concern as kindness. We'd been talking about going to Colombia. It was my suggestion that Odalys visit her country, go to her village anew. So yes, *I* had been talking about going to Colombia. I'd been trying to persuade Odalys. Knowing and feeling are two separate things, and sometimes the complete opposite of each other. I'd said to Odalys that I would finish the thesis and apply for a research project that would enable us to travel. Mathematics, as I said, is not my strong suit—but I see now that this is when Odalys probably decided to be rid of me. I took her encouragement to mean support for my dissertation, and enthusiasm about Colombia. But again I'm trying to find reason where none exists. Odalys had probably been seeing Marat all along. I beg to say that it was not that I objected to another lover, no—I live in the world for god's sake—but I did not want to be surprised by one. Odalys should have stated her preferences at the outset. Marat. I hate his name. I hate how domestic it's become on my tongue. I don't even know this man, and he wasn't hated before, not by me anyway, until Odalys came between him and me. Now Marat settled like a bitter milk in my stomach.

Why had Odalys brought this into my life? I'd been nothing but good to Odalys. Sure, my thesis took up most of my time but I thought Odalys had understood this from the beginning. Here I am again, navel-gazing about what I realize I call wrongly "Odalys' discontent." Odalys was not discontented with me; she was, I must admit finally, beyond me. She had finished whatever it was she'd been doing with me. This I understand now. I must still question: Why introduce this element of hurt called "Marat"? Why not merely tell me that we were at an end? This cruelty, as I will call it, I found unforgivable. Yet I wanted to forgive Odalys, since I loved Odalys. I, however, could not find my way there. And I remain confounded by the mysterious Nkisi who blocked my way out of Odalys' bedroom. I'm not a person who believes in these things, but I'm a person who trusts my own experiences. The Nkisi was fearsome—a being prepared to deploy all of the pain it had ingested, the nails and axe blades and screws and glass and mirrors. If Odalys' cruelty had unleashed the Nkisi, I have no doubt I would've suffered more than this. I wish Marat luck, but perhaps he is a spirit of iron and steel forged in his mechanic's shop, perhaps he is a faithful of Ogun. Still, I have to return to this point: I didn't expect cruelty from someone who looked into my face and told me how she cherished the light she saw there. I simply did not. Can we never trust anyone? *The repetitive structure that I attempt to perform into visibility occurs in a fantasmatic space where we need to examine what is at stake in particular reproductions. In* States of Fantasy, *Jacqueline Rose argues that fantasy is not in opposition to social reality but is actually a precondition of it.*[5]

---

[5] Sharpe/Teoria

For the next months, after the breakup with Odalys, I stayed in my apartment with my papers. I barely went out except to buy potatoes or vegetables or milk. I wish that I found alcohol interesting. It might have helped. This apartment full of its failed paper was all I could love. Luckily it was July and I didn't have to TA. In truth, money was running low. I lived on very little and prayed that the landlord wouldn't raise the rent too much come the fall. Without Odalys, I was reduced to thinking of these domestic things. My thesis, qua thesis, was a pleasure to me. Anyone would think that I found it difficult. Well, I did find it difficult—but not *only* difficult. Sometimes I would lie on the floor among my books and among the reams of paper I'd produced and I would feel a purity. A breathless purity. There was something missing, and this something put a small pall over my pleasures, but nevertheless I could count on my thesis to lift me out. There were no blockages in my way now, I reasoned. Bertolt Auer was dead, Odalys had left me; nothing stood in my way. I'd written the thesis several times over, I merely had to collect the viable parts into a whole that was acceptable to me. Josie Ligna had often said that I didn't understand the administrative aspects of writing a thesis, that I thought it involved pursuing an idea and breaking new ground in thinking, but that really it was all about pacifying the committee and waiting until after to bring any originality to the work itself. She was right, but still I insisted on pressing for originality in the first place. Of course, that is why I haven't had the right approvals signed and the whole matter expedited. I refuse to compromise with idiots. My father always said . . . Well, what's the point of repeating what he said. Odalys has left me.

The light over the mechanic's shop keeps blinking Open, Open, Open, inside an oval turned horizontal. Above, in Odalys' apartment window, stands something I'd never noticed before, a Chinese statue—red and celebratory. There's a Russian doll, too, the kind that obviously iterates itself small and smaller. A mass of plastic flowers, in a huge jar, leans in the left corner of the window frame. I'd never noticed any of this before. The window is packed; a yellowing vine winds its way around and falls dead at the top of the frame. I miss these details; details that end with me wondering what I saw in the first place. My observations are less acute with people than with books.

I sometimes stand across the road looking at Odalys' window at night. Does she see me there, dressed in paper, dressed in the cuts on my fingers from turning pages?

Teoria/Theory

Look, as I said at the start, this is all in the past tense because soon I will hit my fortieth birthday and I decided to make an assessment before going any further. I have been "All But Dissertation" for quite a while, labouring under the title I chose at least eight years ago, "A Conceptual Analysis of the Racially Constructed." You see what I mean. This title took me several years to solidify. I had a great deal of difficulty bringing Bertolt Auer and my then committee around to its efficacy. So much is involved in coming up with a title and a thesis proposal. And as you can imagine, not everyone on the committee could put aside their locations within that title long enough to approve it, let alone want to be part of its execution. What passes for academic argument is so indebted to, yet obscure from, the world as it is and the bodies we live in. There are so many tensions in academia, so many conflictual forces; the academy is a policing institute. It disguises itself with intellectual intention, but it's both superficially and profoundly engaged in the surveillance of intellectual output and ultimately the administration of thought punishment. You'll ask, therefore, why I'm involved in it. That is an easy question to answer. It's reflexive on my part. I blame my father, as his messages were clear from the beginning: make something of myself and don't waste his time or money. When I got to the PhD stage, he was wretched. He said I was wasting my time and should do an MBA, like my brother, and start a business. Capital was all he could see being produced by learning. I'd never admit it to him, but he is correct. This is the true purpose of the academy, to produce layers of managers of capital in one way or another, to carry out and extend the pedagogy of capital.

Sometimes I go around the city and I feel overwhelmed by its inability to free me of the very thing it's supposed to free me of, stasis. I feel tied like a butterfly to a child's string. The skyscrapers don't lift me off the earth the way they're supposed to do. The cars don't speed me away as they promise. The large tractor-trailers crush me on the highway. They crush my spirit with their cargoes of beef and milk. There are so many dead insects like me in their wheel wells.

I haven't said much about the state of the world in these pages, only about my interior world, which is a parody and also a reflection of the real world. My interior world is, Yara might say, an insult to the real world where real people are living and fighting for a real life as I bemoan an incomplete dissertation and failed love affairs. But I'm convinced that people in the real world whose lives are insulted by my moping are also having lousy love affairs that can't be sourced as the reason for how badly life is going. Life is going badly because of where you were born, or whom you were born to, and in between, living from one end of it to the other, we have lousy love affairs. My complaining is inappropriate because of where I was born and whom I was born to. I wasn't born into any bad situation—no teenaged mother, no drunken father, no lecherous uncle, no hard times. Just conformity. Regular, stultifying conformity. I wasn't born into wealth, either. Simply ordinariness. I was born to people who hovered in ordinariness, propping up the rotting system with their desires for wealth and their contempt for people who live in poverty. I'd thought that I could wrench myself out of that dynamic. I thought we all could. But I'm thinking too much, and everyone is going along wherever they are. I have to point out that if the lousy love affair is consistent across these conditions, it must mean that there is another system underlying them, a system that remains untouched by other changes and must therefore be at the root of our unhappiness or disease. Again Gramsci comes to mind.

This reminds me of my earliest love affair with my childhood friend, Iolanta. Iolanta was my dearest friend when I was growing up. She lived in a house with her sister, Myrtle, and brother, Earl, and their mother and father, Mrs. Williams-Torrance and Mr. Torrance, a block away from my house. We went to

Yorkview School together. We walked hand in hand all the way home to Holcolm Road, where Iolanta lived, and Edithvale Drive, where I lived. Sometimes we would walk each other back and forth between houses, Iolanta saying "I'll drop you back" when we arrived at her house, and me saying "I'll drop you back" when we arrived at mine. This went on until one day when Iolanta was about thirteen she became quite ill and had to stay at home. From then on, I only saw Iolanta on Saturdays when I could visit and when Iolanta's parents allowed it. I would bring Iolanta news about this and that, about games and about the new middle school I attended and the new teachers. Iolanta was sad at not being able to go to school anymore. I didn't know what disease Iolanta had. My brother, Wendell, said it was leukemia. Somewhere along Iolanta's illness, Mrs. Williams-Torrance and Mr. Torrance stopped all my visits. Then I would pass by Iolanta's house and stop at her window and call out to her. Iolanta's window was on the second floor, decorated with a dream catcher, and Iolanta would hang out the window waiting for me every morning and every afternoon. When I arrived

I would reach out my arms as if hugging Iolanta, and she would reach out her arms to me. That fall and winter, I would throw Iolanta gum or chocolates or whatever sweets I could find. I became expert at this because if Iolanta's window were to be broken we would both be in trouble. Each morning and every afternoon we would talk like this. In the end, Mrs. Williams-Torrance found out about our talks and put them to an end also. Nevertheless I would pass by and call out Iolanta's name at her window. "Iolanta, Iolanta!" I would sing. No one would appear but I'm a faithful person, I have always been. Even after Iolanta's funeral I still walked by, calling her name.

This part of my life I never refer to. It is only here in these pages that I've attempted to write some of the details. The Williams-Torrances moved away, I suppose because that sad house proved too much for them, but I didn't stop passing by—not until much later, and with regret, and involuntarily. When I left the neighbourhood it was to dismiss my father and his ways, his overbearing voice urging uplift, and to break with my brother, who transformed into my father when he arrived at the age of twenty-five or so.

But Iolanta I mourned well into my twenties. There's a small seam in my brain that contains Iolanta leaning out the window. This image, I think, both beckons and stops me from completing my work. But let me not make excuses or wallow in a long-gone possibility, or be seduced by my indolence, or attach significance to a random albeit formative experience. Who's to say it was formative anyway? In hindsight, I realize I've told that story about a time when days were interminable, so it seems more significant than it is. So much has happened in between, how could it still register as I've told it? Yet I know it accounts for my melancholy, because I now hear, summoned by the memory, Mercedes Sosa singing *Melancolidad* . . . This is why the senses cannot be thoroughly trusted. I could use this incident as the reason that my thesis isn't yet completed; I could attribute my thesis' incompleteness to the incompleteness of my love affair with Iolanta—or, further, the impossibility of that love, since Iolanta's illness intervened and made a separation. This would be fair, I think. Yet, and still—wasn't it the melancholy of the situation that energized the love I felt for Iolanta? Wasn't the melancholy, therefore, the loved thing between Iolanta and me? But I resent that interpretation. Our affections were intense before the melancholy. We played jacks fiercely, we ate pink bubble gum fiercely, we ran to school and back fiercely and we wandered about fiercely, investigating streets and sidewalks, muddy slush and snow. So no, it wasn't melancholy; melancholy came between us.

My intention, which sometimes belies my indolence, is to finish the work this year. Since I'm now free of all encumbrances, since I mean to resolve all the emotional aspects of my life that either get in the way or weigh me down, since there is no lover in the way, I should be able to complete my thesis. I've made a full press on reorganizing the twenty or so disparate chapters that I've written. I'll sort out the various topics that I played with since the death of Bertolt Auer. I'll whittle them down to manageable ideas and then I'll attempt to—no, I *will* bring them into a coherent whole of about six hundred pages. I must also reconstitute my committee. At the moment I've got no standing in the academy, as I was forced to de-enrol due to financial issues. I do hate that word "issues." It is so overused. To be plain, I've run out of money, and in any event it was wasteful to pay a yearly tuition when I was no longer taking courses. My production, vis-à-vis refereed journals, has slowed to one sole-authored essay and one co-authored essay over the last several years. The refereed journals are a racket, notwithstanding.

My apartment is now desolate with the leaves of my thesis. Well truly, my lovers added a certain frisson to the enterprise, a certain urgency, despite the fact that their presences prevented the completion of my work. They would not agree, naturally. Perhaps I used them as a defence against the thesis. I often thought that they helped me to stay in the real world. I thought that I needed them or else I would be swallowed up in the theoretical. But they themselves had their own theories and in the end it's me who was swallowed up each time in each one, without any clarity whatever. Theories ostensibly clarify; theirs did not. Again, you can always look back with jaundice. While I was with Selah and Yara and Odalys, I had no inkling or intention of looking back with rancidity. I hate suggesting that. I swore to myself each time that matters would not end in rancour. It's difficult to keep to this promise, as all I have, or all I can discern that I have, is an apartment cluttered with unfinished thoughts, half-written chapters and a feeling of having wasted a tremendous amount of time in personal dramas. A paragraph of my thesis begins, *We can only see differently if we frame it differently.*[6] I should try to take my own advice. Another paragraph begins, "Often, unknown, unspoken trauma or desire that complicates our lives, increases and reduplicates with every denial and with every repetition."[7] These two beginnings seem to contradict each other, or at least to be in a contrary conversation with each other. Yes, a certain frisson. When I was with them, my lovers, I felt as if my work was important. I was always breaking away from them to do it. They were always interrupting a thought; they always stood in the way of a wider argument, a deeper engagement. I felt then that the important thought lay just a turn of the head away, just a silence that had to be stolen back from attending to my lovers' needs. The

[6] Sharpe/Teoria
[7] ibid

notes I'd quietly made I would reassess in the morn-ings, and each striking revelation was brilliant in the mirror of their adoration of me.

I never finished reading so many texts because of my lovers. The second volume of *Capital*, for instance. Hegel's *Phenomenology of Mind*, though his dismissal of all of Africa was sufficient for me to dis-miss him—nevertheless, Odalys was implicated in this failure. Selah alone stood in the way of all of Lukács—literally, all of Lukács. The half-read texts now lie around my rooms. I can travel to each of the room's hemispheres and find lost theories. I remem-ber which year. I remember which month. These theories nevertheless represent a time in my life, even though I never read them or only half read them, or only paid attention to half of their reasoning. I can't get rid of them. I don't want to get rid of them. I encounter Roland Barthes and I recall Yara com-posing a theatrical piece on sex tourism. "Gide was reading Bossuet while going down the Congo,"[8] Barthes wrote. Gide, you know, was into sex tourism.

---

[8] Barthes

This is a lateral thought because Barthes' piece "The Writer on Holiday" was not about sex tourism but about the "proletarianization of the writer"—a soporific to the proletariat. Or so I read. But I also read sex here, the "sexiness" of the Congo, Gide's libido, the whole of European libidinous enterprise on the African continent. So Barthes invokes Yara and then all I can think of is Yara's artistic inventions in my time with Yara . . . Yara and I are friends, of a sort. We sometimes have tea, but it's not the same as when we were together. All of our being together is contained in references to Barthes. So I can't get rid of Barthes. Someone visiting me would say that my rooms need cleaning. They would see the paper scattered all over the floor, flattened or bunched up, and they would say, Throw this out, for god's sake. I would point to this pile and say, No, I wrote this when Odalys' Nkisi made itself known to me; I wrote this when Selah left. I must keep it all. This way my memories stay intact.

And the books on the stressed shelves? Every one of them contains a memory of mine. I've only to look at Heleith Saffioti's *Women in Class Society* to be invigorated over my mission to finish this work. Her analysis that the "dynamics of the capitalist system in all its phases—mercantile, industrial, financial— led the countries in the most advanced stages of the system to establish an economic structure in the new world that would not hamper the further development of capitalism in the old."[9] This broke apart for me the idea that slave economies in the New World were somehow a relic of earlier economic organization, and it skewered the economic theorists who held that social formations necessarily pass through the vectors of slavery, feudalism and capitalism. To paraphrase. By now anyone who proposes this last theory should have disappeared, but I know that these ideas still lurk cynically. My thesis is to rip them out from their cultural repositories. My first chapter is dedicated—well, in a tangential way, it is dedicated to this ripping out. And so this leads me to Fanon by way of Sylvia Wynter. Wynter says, and I quote, "a mainstream scholar necessarily takes his point of departure from a pre-Fanonian, and thereby purely ontogenetic perspective (with the identity of

---

[9] Saffioti

the human 'us' being seen as a supracultural one defined only by its own); the question that he poses with respect to the possibility of, and a methodology for, an 'objective phenomenology' is the question that in the case of the human, Fanon confronts in his Black Skin/White Masks at the same time as he opens up the possibility of its eventual resolution."[10] Hence Fanon's sociogeny. "Beside philogeny and ontogeny stands sociogeny."[11] As an aside, Wynter is the very meaning of discursive. And why not? Such discursivity I've often been accused of myself. Meaning isn't to be approached with any preconditions, and most assuredly when we're dealing with these matters of being, it is imperative to provide ample caveat and delinquency so that we may arrive at the semblance of a thing. So, no, I don't find Wynter as impenetrable as Josie Ligna has fully confessed she finds her. I wonder how she lives with herself after saying this? What scholarly understanding could she possibly have after such an admission? But

---

[10] Wynter

[11] Fanon

when it comes to social awareness, Josie is much clearer than I. She manages not to get bogged down in meaning as much as I do. There are people for whom theory isn't the source of life or death; it is a commercial object as well as a weapon of hegemony. Josie Ligna has probably already parlayed her skill at this into many jobs. I haven't seen her for a year or so. For me, meaning is a source of life and death. As a result, my TA work has dried up. I insisted that students own their locations in the world. Josie Ligna and others treat students like tabulae rasae, as if civilization has just begun with them, as if they are not culpable. I insist on an ethical relation to the present rooted in an authentic one to the past. Well, fine. I have forfeited teaching gigs for my pedagogy. I retreat to my paper rooms, my paper floors, my paper walls. I won't fight for what I deserve, for what by right and by any measure of intelligence I should have as a matter of course, as a matter of the obvious. This is when they, whoever *they* are, reduce you.

My father used to say, calling up from the bottom of the stairs to my brother, Wendell, and me, "You may plot and plan but you cannot bring down the government of this house." He was a tyrant, and so the way I figure it, I've already met the worst. They must have cratered him in Sheffield, where he took a degree in mechanical engineering. But Academia will not make me cower. My father would command my brother and me to sit in silence for the hours of Sunday afternoon between one and three. We couldn't fall asleep or even read a book. He said this was a lesson in discipline. Sunday, between the hours of one and three, are precisely the hours when one wants to fall asleep. If he found us eyeing each other and smiling, he would make us face the wall and prohibit us from turning our heads. "Say your times tables in your head," my father would advise. "Think of all the starving children in the world." Also, he would counsel, "Prepare your thoughts for the coming week—obedience and brightness are your goals." We would stand there facing the wall, my brother incubating an anger he would take out on me when he could, slapping me behind the head as my father would slap him; and me plotting my father's overthrow through small, wicked acts. For the most part, to be truthful, I went under the radar of my father. My brother, Wendell, bore the brunt, as he was a boy. Once, in defence of Wendell, I placed a small tack in one of my father's brown Derby shoes. When he cried out in pain, it was with the strangest sound. A plaint, so surprised. This wasn't the sound I wanted, I realized. It was a childish sound. His pain, I realized, wasn't the key to his overthrow—not his physical pain, at any rate. He sounded helpless. People in power should not sound helpless, I thought; they have no right to sound helpless. This route, then, would not overthrow my father. It would have to be something else, something less personal. It would have to be about something he wanted, since *getting* was my father's first principle. Wanting and getting. That is when I decided to remove myself as soon as possible from his governance. My father needed subjects, instruments that he could move around, order around, send for and send away.

You'll notice that I have not mentioned my mother in this account. At least, I don't think that I have so far. My mother was a ghost who lived in the house. She did as my father ordered. She did this out of utter fidelity to him; she loved him. She loved him to her extinction. Your father says and your father wants and your father knows, and your father will and your father won't. These were the salutations at the beginning of each of her sentences. Her affinities for my brother and me were predicated on my father's approval. We were each schooled by her in ways of being. My brother can speak for himself. But I think that there are people like my mother trapped in imaginaries. I do not mean her own imagination because I don't think that she made the whole thing up herself. When I was a child, I used to watch my mother apply makeup to her face and neck. She mistook my fascination for pleasure and camaraderie. All the time, as she applied, she instructed me in the right amount of eyeliner, the right amount of eyeshadow, the scintilla of rouge, the basalt of foundation cream, which held all this up; the realgar mineral of lipstick at the death. I saw her *appear*—another person, whom she represented as herself. Her eyes encouraged me to imitate her practices. But even when I was a child, these appearances of my mother disturbed me. I was not the only one. I observed my father's response at this transformation. He became obsequious. The more foreign she became the more obsequious he. I say *became* but I am not sure about that verb. It was more like an emergence of what my mother thought was her true self. This made me think later that there was a Plato's cave of gender that my mother and father inhabited, and I was their clear-eyed philosopher. My mother tried to usher me into this cave with her enactments of femininity; I was unable to see anything but weakness in that invitation. I felt as if she were asking me not to be the person I knew myself to be. When she had control of me, she forced me into the display; then, I was her possession to be dressed up in uncomfortable shoes and garish fuchsia outfits. She would lead me down streets and into churches and stores and social gatherings as if I were a pet on display, like her. At ten she recommended band-aids for my nipples. I had not noticed them as a problem. At twelve she laid out her jewellery on the bed offering me a bangle if I *behaved* like a girl. I found her syntax interesting in the use of the subjunctive—as if she were not describing known objective facts, but a concept, a person she observed, rightly, unconnected to present and past time.

One might say I am being harsh about my mother and father. I'm not being harsh; I am being analytic. I'm being frank. Frankness about the people who bring you into the world is never appreciated. I believe that I am describing them as they are, not as sentiment or social script would have me do. Again someone might remark on the stereotypic patriarchal portrait I've painted of them both. They are as I have described. If they are not differentiated in my portrait, it's because each of them had drunk from the same draught of patriarchy and found it intoxicating—to this day most likely. They're compelled by this force; they acquiesce to this force and they acquire power through it. No one wants to give up this lurid power. One might argue that in this complex my mother wasn't powerful, but I would argue that she, however delusional, saw herself as powerful. The aesthetic of brutality, which produces women's bodies as desire and romance, captured her. She lived in a false consciousness, and still inhabits it now. I can't say that this mask of hers, or what I'll call a mask, ever slipped. She was fully taken up in it.

My brother tells me I'm too harsh with her. Again this word, "harsh." I can't take him seriously anymore. How can he see what I see, when he too has adopted his position as patriarch, duplicating what oppressed him in our childhood? It could be that given his sex, he made an easy immersion into his gender role; given mine, transition out of the gender role ascribed was my only chance at sovereignty. I suppose he and I despised different things in my father. I despised my father's authoritarianism, his dominance. My brother despised our father's indifference toward him, his disdain. As I've said, meaning is a source of life and death to me.

My father loved Pimm's and oranges—leftover from his Sheffield days. He had a drink of this each Sunday morning. Sunday mornings would begin with this harmony—my father and my mother in the kitchen drinking a Pimm's cup with oranges. Despite the way Sundays would end for my brother and me, they always began in peace. Every Sunday morning, I'd forget my father's routine of spoiling Sundays with his disgruntled persona. This routine made our winters even duller than they would have been.

But I recall how each spring morning, I'd lie in my bed looking up at the April-May light searing the air with its soft laser. I would lower my eyelashes to a curtain and play with opening and closing the aperture of my eyelids. I would hear my mother singing in the kitchen and I would hear the laughter of my father mixed with the smell of eggs, bacon and fresh bread. And I would hear the quiet of Sunday buttressing this. My father was always in a good mood at the beginning of this day. He would squeeze oranges into a huge glass jug with ice, mixing his own and my mother's with Pimm's, and mine and Wendell's with slices of cucumber. Then, with the lilac tablecloth on the table, the teacups and saucers and Sunday plates sitting prettily, the bread steaming with butter, the world was peaceful. Even my father seemed peaceful. If only Sundays did not proceed. If only they lingered on their early hours. I never knew when the turn would come. It was like the aura before a migraine, triggered by a certain heaviness, an odour of cleaning product from my mother's kitchen, too acute. Then the living room became a torture chamber. This was after my mother and father returned home from church with my brother and me in tow, ordering us to clean shoes, lay out clothing for Monday and bring finished homework to the living room for inspection. Then Sunday was lost. Or that part of the day I called Sunday. So I don't do Sundays well. I don't know what to do with myself on a Sunday. I've tried all my adult life to recuperate Sunday, and I've been unsuccessful. I've made a promise to myself to finish my work on a Saturday so that the following day I'd be completely free from the history and memory of those unfortunate Sunday afternoons.

Despite my state of no money to speak of, I'm determined to press on. There are few itinerant jobs out there that will hire a forty-year-old—perhaps those hundreds of little boutique coffee shops rising up that hire people called baristas. God knows where all this coffee is coming from. My inability, it would seem, to get along with people has put me at a disadvantage with regard to work. The only position I've been able to get, on and off, is at the university's writing centre, where I help first-years cobble together a decent paper on children's literature or human geography, or on energy and society, or on Being Human: Classic Thought on Self and Society. I won't disparage the students who come to the writing centre. If I do, I'll find myself out of work again. Whenever I launch a critique against anything, anything, I feel obliged to take a political and principled position— and then, of course, though my ethics remain intact, my livelihood becomes precarious. This time I'll have to keep my mouth shut until the thesis is written. Don't think that I don't hear the desultory notes I'm registering here. This time of reassessment is by necessity a doldrums. It is as if I am swimming in the Sargasso Sea, and seaweed has washed up in my apartment. I'm making my way through the sea creatures and I am trying to find the flowers of the sargassum. The problem with not having a lover is that there is no distraction from the person I am. There is no one who needs my counsel and advice. There's no one to fix, in other words, except me. I'll say this last before anyone says it for me.

I don't think that I was trying to fool my lovers. As I said from the beginning, I merely thought that my lovers would give me respite from the worries of my thesis. I thought they would give me a view on the world that would attenuate my gloom. And truthfully, they did. I loved being with them. I made myself useful where I could. If that meant giving advice, certainly I gave advice. I'm not one to coddle people. I'm not one to patronize. Though . . . wasn't that, in fact, what I did in all cases? I must be honest. But that time was that time, and now I really don't need another person in my life. It's so disconcerting when one's ideas, one's view of the world doesn't coincide with one's actual life. But as I said, I will be diligent about examining this.

This thesis will attempt to show some aspects of the con-stitutive whole. . . . What are the unabstracted and real relations that are lived out every day? This thesis is only a preliminary study and perhaps as such it will prove the basis for further study.[12] I've gone back and forth on that last sentence. It smacks of a false modesty. This is not a preliminary study in the least. I've spent many years on this proposition. I'm not sure how this modesty will be understood. I may be laughed at, given how long it's taken me to complete my thesis. Some may

---

[12] Teoria

think that I'm hedging my bets, afraid of the deluge of criticism that I am sure will follow. On the other hand, it could be a meaningfully rude gesture on my part, suggesting that if this great work is preliminary, I challenge anyone to top it. The cross-disciplinarity of the work is breathtaking, if I say so myself. In it, I've cited architecture, literature and semiotics. I believe that I've made intelligible for the first time the theory of instrumentality and longing. And the image of women in painting from antiquity to the nineteenth century—let me not fail to mention the great John Berger here—I've scattered throughout, with brief exegeses on them in order to illustrate my point about the complete absence of theorizing the male body. When I say theorizing, I mean that it has never been the body in question. The female body has been gone over, it has been done to death. I don't mean any pun here, but it is indeed a dead body, an embalmed corpse that is shuttled out as ancient priests might in some bizarre ceremony for an ancient relic. Our gaze should light now on the male body, its location and its excesses. Theory has failed so far to witness the spec-tacle of the masculine. Theory has merely assumed the spectacle of the masculine as a priori. Theory has fallen down in rooting out this ubiquitous being that commands everything but appears nowhere, is fed and nurtured on a corpse, and requires more and more feeding. So the female body is placed on the pyre every day, roasted and dressed to enliven this necrophiliac. Who is at the centre of this body, how is it constituted, how is it hidden from observation; who enforces this regimen of necrogenesis? This is my line of inquiry. Simply, who is the being that feeds off the corpse of femininity? My chapter is therefore called "Male Bodies: Eating the Dead." Some will think that I've gone too far. I think that I haven't gone far enough. Bertolt Auer never liked this chapter. It made him uncomfortable. I understood why. We had a prolonged argument about what I call the excess of the male body. My view, I told him, was that the male body was the unregulated body in the context of regulations imposed on bodies qua bodies; that the male body was hidden in its excess; that it overreached, leaked as existence. Auer could not grasp what I was coming at theoretically, and so he became defensive, as if I were speaking of *his* body, his *personal* body.

I tried to say—because after all he was a philosopher—
that I was problematizing a thematic, a paradigm, a
quality, if not the dominant quality, of being. "Being," I
said, "is constituted as male and I'm trying to untangle
the ontogenic and the philogenic and to propose a
sociogenic in Fanon's terms as regards the male." Auer
wasn't usually so reticent. At least, not when it came to
expatiating on *being*. He would have involved Heidegger
here, but he couldn't collect his tongue from the floor.
I continued: By "excess" I mean that this body, the one
we are problematizing, its wants, its desires and its
needs, are taken as given. As natural. And therefore
these desires, wants and needs are never brought
under scrutiny or reined in. It is, in fact, the male body
that is biology. I know this sounds counterintuitive,
given feminist theories that posit, I would say rhetori-
cally, that it's the female body that is treated as solely
biology. No, I say it's the male body that's marked as
unsociable, as unable to be brought into society or
brought under the regulations of the social or the
political. What I call its excess—that is, the way this
body's "biology" supersedes the social and resists
socialization—is the focus of my examinations. If

socialization is the process of humans coming into society, coming into the social, why are men excused from this task? And why do we call it society if we exempt the excess of the male body from coming under the breadth of its possible processes? Auer, and by way of Auer, Heidegger, takes this state as a priori.

Auer, if not Heidegger, blew up when I said this.

"Auer," I said, "I am not you; this is what you fail to see. And for that matter, you're not you, if in fact the you that you think you are is without history, and in that, like me. I refuse your starting point. It's arbitrary, vague, deliberately vague and generalizing."

The day of that argument, Auer finally opened his office door and directed me out. His face was a strange colour. He was silent. "But let me continue," I said without moving. "By excess I mean it's the thing we never speak of. It is sediment we never disturb, we never address. If it's addressed, a brutal response is applied. The only reason for women's subjugation and negation, I'd say, is the sustenance of this unspeakable." This was the last argument I had with Auer. Much as I hated him, I certainly hope that it did not contribute to his ill health and subsequent end. Whatever I've said about him here, I didn't wish him dead. Not in the physical sense. Only his ideas, his modernity. I will say no more. I don't want to descend into hypocrisy. And my chapter has outlived him, and will continue to outlive him. I want to return to this idea of *excess*. I'll put it in capital letters. EXCESS. I want to say that the leakage, the *overproduction*, of masculinity is at least responsible for the dreadful violence in the world. Yes, I quite like that concept—the overproduction of masculinity. Just as one may overproduce a certain commodity and then find oneself with its overgrowth or decay. This excess then becomes the state of affairs, the state of being, and the very production of being. Certainly, as a parenthetical, there are masculinities. The idea I'm referring to is plural, and not all masculinities, or not all areas of those masculinities, produce, in and of themselves, excess. I feel I'm appeasing Auer here, so let me banish that last notion. Because as we live today, none of this is disrupted, shaken loose by—as useful as they might be— theories of radical thought that unearth and contest hegemony. These theories subtend the excess.

Everyone retreats into this excess when a critique is launched. They retreat into this excess as "being."

Eliding what might be into what is. There's a certain cowardice to this, a mendacity. Half of us know that we'll be killed if we provide a sustained attack on the overproduction of masculinity, and half of us will be the killers. I say "us" only out of habit. There is no "us." Another elision. Who am I, then, if I'm not Bertolt Auer? I am the being who recognizes Bertolt Auer and who shocked Bertolt Auer into recognition. It might have caused his death. It's not for me to say.

This reminds me of Nawal El Saadawi's *Death of an Ex-Minister*. In it, the ex-Minister falls ill and dies because a woman looks him directly in his eyes. Or, one could summon Adorno's *Metaphysics*. Auer himself, were he to take his theories to their obvious indications, would quote Adorno: "I would say, not that evil is trivial, but that triviality is evil—triviality, that is, as the form of consciousness and mind that adapts itself to the world as it is, that obeys the principle of inertia. And this principle of inertia truly is what is radically evil."

Anyway, I'll stop here. When I begin to talk out my ideas before committing them to paper, by the time I get to my desk the ideas have slipped me. Often I'd begin to tell Selah a thought, and her silence would lead me to think how important the idea was, and so I would talk and talk over dinner or on our evening neighbourhood walks, and then when we returned home I'd have lost my train of thought. Then I would ask Selah to reprise my thoughts for me, and she would say, "——, I can't talk the way you do. You said something about some guy." This would disappoint me and infuriate me. *Some guy?* As always, she was right. It was about some guy. I would sit at my desk and try to recuperate my ideas that had felt so generative when I was telling Selah, but which now, at my desk, seemed derivative because Selah had astutely précised them into "some guy." There was an acuteness to Selah; she could condense a thought of mine into its irrelevance. But Selah thought that every idea that didn't involve her beauty was a waste of time. How much time had I spent trying to convince her otherwise? Hoping that she would adopt my language, my way of seeing the world? At the same time, I valued Selah's way of looking at the world and I didn't want that to change. I don't want to revisit my life with Selah. I can't be certain of my interpretation, and it would be better not to skewer any views of that past. I haven't spoken to Selah since our breakup. I haven't seen her since the day I put my belongings in a rented car and sped away, singing. It wasn't really down a highway; it was across town. If I were to add up the notes I kept when I was with Selah, they would be a deluge. Completely incomprehensible notes, but a deluge. I have to make a bold decision regarding their indecipherable language: Keep them or throw them away? For the moment, I've stuffed them into two ottomans, as each time I get ready to throw them out I'm swept away by a nostalgia for the thought itself discernible in the note. This thought had a life; it was once accompanied by supporting evidence. Then I look at another thought, written in another note, and recognize it as something so recondite, so epicurean, yet so ephemeral that even if I could recuperate it, this thought wouldn't have a life in the world of brutalism I now inhabit. So I visit the otto-mans as one visits a library—simply for the hints and the references, for inspiration. I can't throw these notes out. The Ottoman Files, I joke about them. I imagine them going on in their life as I imagine the set of ideas of a separate culture; this one inhabiting the thoughts of these sets of people, the other inhabiting another—all of them existing in a parallel universe. Others may see a messy rubbish dump when they open my door; I see the great propositions I've written, the breathing room I've made between myself and the dread.

When my brother, Wendell, came to see me a year ago, his face registered increasing horror with each step through the hallway. I thought: how people change. How people conform to the most grim manifestations of the human. It's truly amazing. His room in my parents' house used to be a pigsty—not of paper like this, but of pizza boxes and stinking socks and porn magazines under his mattress. There were cups unreturned to the kitchen for weeks, growing colonies of fungus and spiders. Now he hesitates in my apartment as if he's seen something terrifying. I showed him the alleyway through my books toward the kitchen, but he backed away toward the front door saying he had to have a smoke and wouldn't want to cause a fire. I agreed and followed him out. He didn't deserve to be among my precious books and paper. I told him this as we stood on the sidewalk. He said, "Are you alright?"

I said, "Don't bullshit me, what do you want?"

He said, "Nothing. Why can't I come to see you?"

I said, "Why would you leave your downtown posh condo to come to my dump?"

He said, "For god's sake, you're sounding fucking crazy. And you're right, that apartment is a dump. Shit, why don't you move home?"

"Home?" I said, "Home? Now who's sounding crazy?"

"Well," he said, "father and mother could use some help. They're not getting younger, you know." It was my turn to look incredulous.

"You're out of your fucking mind," I said. "Look," I said, "I'm trying to work on my diss. What fucking shit are you bothering me for?"

"We used to talk about a lot of things," he said. "Why don't we anymore?" Christ, I thought, he's having a crisis of some kind and I can't deal right now. He sat down on the sidewalk and smoked. So I sat down beside him.

"You've chosen what you've chosen," I said finally. "Yeah," he said. "You're lucky."

We talked like this, my brother and I, when we were alone. Short, staccato, colloquial affectations—in homage to our incipient teenaged rebellion. We sat there that night for a while, smoking. I don't even smoke. But I smoked with my brother. Yes, he chose what he chose, and yes, I'm lucky. "Well, fuck," I said. "Well, fuck," he said. I don't know what time it was when we got up and I went inside and he went his way. I could always sit in silence with my brother for a long time. He's the only person I could do that with. Ever since our childhood. And it gave me a peace to sit on the sidewalk with him, even though the evening had started out with my annoyance with him. We sat in my luck and his choice. Anyone else, I would've said, "I'm not lucky. You chose, I chose." But I allowed my brother the balm of thinking I was lucky and that he had fallen into some hard thing. We sat there for hours. People came into the building and people left. We talked until no one came in and no one left. A little drizzle fell and then it stopped. If we talked, it was only because he brought up *The Alienist* by Machado de Assis and we both laughed. My brother loved Machado de Assis. He half-learned Portuguese to read Machado de Assis in the original. He devoured anything by Machado de Assis. *Philosopher or Dog?*, *Dom Casmurro*. I think he talked about Machado de Assis that night in order to live for a while with his true passion. In *The Alienist*, there's a doctor who returns from Europe to a small town in Brazil and begins putting everyone who doesn't conform into an asylum. Then, changing his theory about who's mad, he releases them and he puts everyone who conforms into the asylum. And then finally, on further development of his theory, he lets those people out and puts himself, alone, into the asylum. My brother loved this novella; he loved the doctor, Simão Bacamarte. My brother had been in the middle of his PhD on Machado de Assis when my father finally got to him. But maybe my brother always wanted my father to get to him. "You're in the asylum," I said to him. He laughed out loud; his shoulders shook. He said, "You're in the asylum." We both laughed for a long time. Maybe I was in the asylum too. I loved my brother. It must've been four in the morning when we stopped smoking and got up from the sidewalk. I watched him get into his car. He waited for me to go into the doorway. He left. What a strange evening that was.

Such ritualistic ceremonies differ dramatically from popular culture performances of sexualized female bodies . . . with disparate cultural performances yielding relatively the same outcomes across. . . . I am especially interested, what I find important to this dissertation are the eruptions and repetitions yet unremarked upon in previous work.[13] It seems to me that the world would have been different if my brother, Wendell, had completed his thesis. I don't know why I say this, since he wasn't about to discover or solve some great scientific mystery—but I feel his seemingly small act of conformity to power set time back. All acts of conformity to power set time back. They set back thinking. A minute, subatomic change would've occurred in how social relations are perceived and extended had the regimen of power been disrupted. An anomaly would have occurred in the power grid. And therefore the course of human history may have changed because

---

[13] Sharpe/ Teoria

of this small act. My brother's life may also have been different. How, I can't say. I won't propose the term "happier," since life is so changeable on the micro level, on the day to day. Yet, as I said, so unchangeable in the macro. He might've set off a time bomb in the unchangeable, nevertheless. I don't say this to boast—but I believe that my positioning, my stance as I've outlined so far, represents an explosion, however subatomic, in the networks of power that obviate a life truly lived. My apartment represents the living archive of this life. Meanwhile, my brother thinks that I am lucky and he thinks my apartment is a dump. All that indecipherability on the floor, my walls of books, my piles of paper—I appear crazy to him, yet he thinks I'm lucky.

Now I'm more determined to finish this thesis, even though it involves the gargantuan task of bringing all that I've thought into a monumental work. I feel that I should eschew the traditional coherent work of propositions and proofs, supporting documents and footnotes. If Benjamin can do it, so can I. If Barthes can do it, so can I; and certainly if Foucault can do it, so can I. *All of the works engage with the immediately chromatic category of race as race replaces and/or coincides with questions of hegemony, historicity, and class, and conquest, to render these previously invisible categories visible.*[14] This seems to me a good starting point for chapter three, where I deal with artists such as Benjamin-Constant and Delacroix, who, counter to other assertions, visibilize race, only to spectacularize it. If their art is art at all, which I dispute (I say it is "yellow journalism," not art), it's the art of spectacle—of spectacularizing these bodies as outside of the human. *The eruptions and repetitions of this visibilization foreclosed any address to the human, added to which a vocabulary of seeing was produced; an alphabet, if you will, of the look. Liberty led the people over the body of the women of Algiers.*[15] I know that it will be difficult to get this wide and multi-layered reading through my new committee, when I form the committee. I'm positive they'll say that I should focus on one thing or another. The problem with these people is they

---

[14] Sharpe/Teoria
[15] Teoria

have no concept of history or time. For someone such as me, everything must be done in one shot. I'll never have another chance to elaborate these ideas. It's not merely a question of my age but of the urgency of the task and the material conditions. These last militate against ideas such as mine erupting on the surface of the intellectual discourses that are constantly at work dampening down such ideas. We all know what I'm talking about, but the committee will pretend not to understand. I'll have to insist. *Again I am concentrating on these works as they obsessively reproduce and repeat across time and space, the morality plays of the colonialists and imperialists. They force us daily to re-enact these dramas in literature and art as if we were first-grade children learning the alphabet.*[16]

My critics, like that deplorable man who writes for the newspapers, will say that I am describing a world that they don't recognize. Well, patently that is true. I'm describing a world that I am forced to live in and they aren't. I'm describing a world that is constructed

---

[16] Teoria

through their unseeing. I refer here, as evidence, to the time I was asked by a daily newspaper to write for their series about the birth of the city two hundred years ago. It was Josie Ligna who gave my name to the editor she knew at the daily. Naturally, I wrote of the poverty of the city, the shelters that were underfunded; I said that the fact that we need shelters at all is the travesty. A columnist at the paper decided to chastise me in the next issue for telling a lie about the city, and for only highlighting the grim and ignoring the progress. He was dissatisfied that immigrants who no longer expressed the values of the former colonists had overrun the city. He eulogized on the loss of certain principles—really, certain stereotypes—of the hardworking and the puritan. Christ, this city is full of dreadful people. I couldn't ignore him. I sent a letter to the editor, a letter longer than the essay I'd written, lambasting and parodying his upstanding colonists/settlers who had suddenly been overrun by the colonized and the ungrateful. Were I of a violent type, I would wish that sort of person to be assassinated. He is proof of how quickly the system can galvanize itself to counter even the slightest uptake of air by the oppressed. He's the embodiment of a gag.

I suspect now that Josie Ligna had recommended me knowing that I would be attacked, and not at all because—as she said—she felt that "other" voices should be heard. She'd become known as a public intellectual and was called upon to pontificate on all matters urban. I was flattered by her recommendation at the time, and here's my weakness, again. For all my alertness, I'm vain. I should've told Josie Ligna to do it herself. After all, doesn't she live in the same city that I do? Isn't she implicated, doesn't she feel the discomfort as I do? If indeed we want the same world, I needn't be the one to speak as if I possess a special legitimacy. She needs to say how the injustices affect her. In this way I was vulnerable to this viper's attack. I don't mind, though, and I'm not afraid of defending my ideas. Naturally, a possible source of income was prematurely cut off because of my relentless attack on the columnist. I'd hoped that the editor would solicit more pieces from me, but he took offence at my rightful repudiation of the idiot. He published an edited version of my letter, leaving out the most salient points about gravestones needing to be cut from lead to keep down the stench of the dreadful civilization the columnist represented.

A variety of fantasies are worked out in the colonized bodies in each of the paintings of Benjamin-Constant and Delacroix.... "the force in the real world of the unconscious dreams of nation," Jacqueline Rose writes in her work on Bessie Head's A Question of Power. *I would elaborate, the all-too-conscious dreams of Empire, not to say the realities of empire are at work in* Benjamin-Constant *and* Delacroix. *Scholars have remarked in a cursory fashion on the statements of these two. "How pitiful it is to see how you live, how enjoyable to paint it," said Benjamin-Constant. "If I have won no victories for my country, at least I can paint for it," said Delacroix. Well then, with what joy indeed did they set about the task of impressing themselves on the project of conquest in their work, we must ask. And we must answer with every fibre. With every fibre we must tell the truth of their artistic exploits. Instead we praise the realgar, exalt the verdigris, remark on the brush strokes of the carbon black. What Benjamin-Constant and Delacroix make visible is that project of conquest and colonization. In both their statements, the former following the latter by some forty years or so, we read the imperial, the patriotic and the libidinal, the abjection. Their apologists have muted these political statements and, worse, they have elided these statements into the rhetoric of art for art's sake. A term we must abhor and eviscerate. These painters were well aware of their ambitions' outcomes. Their desires coincided with a vision of the world that they set out to commit to canvas. More than "introducing the inhabitants of North Africa to Western painting," as one scholar equivocates, these paintings introduce the inhabitants of North Africa to the gaze of abjection. Moreover the paintings curate the object(ification) of those bodies; their thingification or fetishization.[17]*

When I've gathered all of my ideas, when I've brought them into being fully, the manuscript will be about seven hundred pages or so. That is, when I've crystallized all the material lying here in my rooms. Notwithstanding, there will still be at least twenty-one hundred pages of notes remaining for later work. But I feel that the committee won't be able to assess that length of a work, and despite the temptation to

---

[17] Teoria

overwhelm them, I must draw back and get through this now. I feel the urgency of the moment—and circumstance has already forced me to delay. Selah and Yara and Odalys no longer account for my tardiness; at least I can no longer blame them. I mean, I never blamed them per se—after all, one has to live one's life. But my life was never meant to be tied up. No, I despise this description. If it had worked out with any of them—But what can we mean by "worked out"?—if I'd managed not to disappoint them, or they me . . . Well, these propositions are neither here nor there. I live a life of the mind—or I flatter myself that I do. Even if it only amounts to self-involvement, it would seem as if I'm happy living this way.

Odalys always said that I lived too much in my head. She said I had no body, she said that I walked around her place like a floating brain. Teoria, she called me. One would have thought that she would've kept me, then, as part of her occult accoutrement. I never hear from Odalys and I never pass by Affinity Street without trepidation. I don't dare knock on Odalys' door in case her Nkisi answers. There's little that I fear more than that nail-ridden figure that blocked my way in and out of Odalys' rooms. I return to Odalys here because recently she's been in my dreams and I can't help but think this isn't coincidence. Odalys does not appear by accident, not even in dreams. Some would think that my attention to this aspect of Odalys leaves me open to charges of superstition, or belies my much vaunted commitment to dialectical materialism. They would be wrong on both fronts. I'm not in the least bit superstitious. Odalys put ideas out in the air and these ideas are taken up and enacted. Odalys, in this way, is like any politician or preacher—the force of those ideas enacted became the fact of those ideas. If Odalys could walk backwards without damage, and if Odalys could find me and know from my face that I was wasting my light, then Odalys' way had a legitimacy. Whether I believe in Odalys' spiritism or not, her apprehension was correct. I'll always love Odalys for that moment of recognition. The emotional facts between us are as important as the social or political facts. So when I remember Odalys, I remember that day when she saw me. Though I hope her presence in my dreams is not meaningful. She's appeared there far too frequently of late. I hope that Odalys isn't trying to make a comeback.

In this chapter, I will foreground the effects and confusions of the enactments of race, class, and sex passing in Gertrude Stein's "Melanctha." As this chapter engages the ways that Stein produces meaning through the use of variously (en)coded and re-racinated black and white, female, and feminized bodies, I will also situate the problems involved in reading ethnographically as, I argue, that Stein uses black bodies and approximated linguistic styles, simplifying the characters and their behaviours in ways that are largely reducible to assumed racial traits. In a letter to Mabel Weeks, Stein wrote, "I am afraid that I can never write the Great American Novel. I don't know how to sell on a margin or to do anything with shorts and longs, so I have to content myself with —— [here Stein used a racial epithet I will not repeat] and servant girls and the foreign population generally."

In order to write the displaced but distinctly "American" novel, Stein must first write herself out by reworking and displacing lesbianism, Jewishness, and familial estrangement onto other bodies. "Melanctha" is the trace that Stein leaves behind precisely so that we can locate her as analogously other. It is what she declared she must expunge in order to write the great American novel; to complete her self-transformation she also writes her way to whiteness. For Stein, black-face is a way to work out questions of "taboo sexuality" and representational parricide—it is a representational medium that allows her to displace these problematics onto black people. In other words, she uses blackface to get from black people the "stuff" of nothingness: the medium of transformation. Indeed, the effect of "Melanctha" is decidedly not the undoing of naturalist narrative about black people, but the inscription of a different (racialist) narrative, or different narrativizations, within what remains a largely naturalist paradigm. "Melanctha," though, is read by audiences that continue, one might say in order to continue, to confer upon Stein ethnographic authenticity. This despite knowledge that in the context of Stein's world, "Melanctha" is both a production of and productive of her style and her working through personal dilemmas and literary styles—it is, within her own "semiotics," an anti-naturalist attempt. At the same time her representations of black people are persistently viewed as

accurate and perceptive—in short, as naturalistically,
ethnographically authentic.[18]

I must pull this thesis together "irregardless," as my father says. All my life I've sat at an angle observing the back and forth of other people's lives. I dare say I sit at this angle toward my own life. I must get up from these rooms of mine and get going with life. Life is not lying down in a litter of paper. I've got so much more to do. I have sufficient material for a lifetime of theory. The work energizes me. Always. Each time I return to it, I'm opened up anew to just how much it's become necessary to any future living. Not simply for my own small life but for the lives of others. I anticipate overturning sclerotic structures of thinking with the completion of this work.

[A]nd while I recognize that certain radical theorists of diaspora (like Gilroy, Davies, Hall, and Walcott) have attempted to problematize these sorts of passionate attachments through the very idea of diaspora, I maintain throughout this chapter that diasporic discourses generally rely on powerful notions of "homeland" and

---

[18] Sharpe/Teoria

ethnicity/race. . . . My argument in this section is essentially that Xavier Simon's novel(s) indicates but ultimately overwhelms the discourse of diaspora because it consciously subverts and abandons the object that manages to endure uncritically in many diasporic discourses: the "homeland" from which one is exiled.

The oceanic is the site of an unutterable trauma; . . . the oceanic also, with its unpredictable currents and intensities, evokes the stream-of-consciousness techniques that Xavier Simon frequently uses in her writings. Finally, as Spillers acutely notes in psycho-social terms, the oceanic is a liminal zone, where existing social and symbolic orders are in abeyance; in the space of the oceanic. From this liminal space, radically new inscriptions of body and sexuality can be explored. . . . Along these lines, it is crucial to note that . . . stereotypical depictions of a racialized or gendered body are notably absent in the novel; and, in contrast, depictions of the revolutionary energies of the body are almost always accompanied by the rupture or displacement of docile or domesticated bodies.[19]

---

[19] Chariandy/Teoria

I think of Selah and Yara and Odalys now, not as hindrances, not even as transit points to myself or as the lessons of my life—but as the life itself, the theory of my life. They and I are not made of nothingness. They've gone on in their own narratives. I've gone on in mine. I must sit in the knowledge of them; we remain adjacent. They've given me, in part, material for a lifetime of theory, but I can't live in the prosthetic. They are not my arms, not my body, nor my head, not even my imagination—they escape and exceed me and I'm left with me.

I have every feeling that I'll acquire a post at a university and the funding to continue my work. I would even settle for a college. Come to think of it, a college would be much better. That's where I'll be of the most help. I must gather my ideas. I must sit in the knowledge of my possibilities and impossibilities. The pleasures of returning to the page and the work take me over. I will inhabit the fullness within the limits. It's a logic I can live with. Here we go then, Teoria.

First, as a starting point . . .[20]

---

[20] All subsequent references to this text will be made parentheti-
cally. This raises questions about what is "consensual" and how con-
sent is always complicated by class, race and sex. There has been a
court battle over ownership of the piece. I do not yet know who has
won the case. See Coco Fusco, "The Other History of Intercultural
Performance," *English Is Broken Here* (1995). As filmmaker Charlene
Gilbert pointed out in conversation with me, the things that signify
otherness in the video are derived from . . . Sharpe/Teoria, op. cit.

I must say here without equivocation . . .[21]

---

[21] RWW/Teoria.

The Sublime Object of Ideology (1989) and Looking Awry (1991) seem to enter western scholarship as a way to think politics, culture and cultural products in new and exciting ways. Žižek's insightful readings of Marxism, European critical theory, psychoanalysis and Hitchcock offered us an exciting intellectual exercise in cultural study that was both similar to and exceeded what we were calling cultural studies at the time. I even used his phrase "nation enjoyment" from Looking Awry to coin the term "nation thing" as a way to speak to what diaspora as a concept allowed Black people to get at beyond national concerns.

Žižek so quickly became a darling of the western academic elite that it is difficult to pinpoint the moment where his incisive critique turned to caricature of himself. I like to think that too many forums with Judith Butler did him in. The decline was fast and now it seems totally complete. Asked to comment on all sorts of things, Žižek's scholarly trajectory is a parable for not saying, "No, I can't." His ideas on race, identity and gender in the last years have betrayed an intellectual cul de sac, a man unable to think outside of the masculine scholarly frame of the all-knowing intellectual. His contributions can now be read as a parody of what he does not know, and what he shoved into what he once knew, but with no synthesis, only condescending ignorance. His newspaper columns bear this point out most forcefully and sadly.

Regarding my father . . .[22]

---

[22] Not much has been said here about my father except that
which reflects my utter resentment of him. When that started,
I have explained only tangentially. He was not always who he
became, I am told. None of us are who we become. For most of my
childhood he was a distant and domineering figure. You will say all
fathers are. I only place this note here to say that he may not have
been adequately represented in my account, since my knowledge of
him is based on extant references that are not sufficient to lay out
his psychologies. I am therefore only left with my resentments and
my brief readings of his life in reference to me. In passing, I will say
that he and my mother met in Sheffield, where he was doing a
mechanical engineering degree and my mother was staying with a
relative who worked at the Sheffield hospital until she could make
her own way. Apparently they met on a bus and that was that.
I invoke them here in this thesis neither as narrative, nor as trauma,
but as epistemology.

ACKNOWLEDGEMENTS

Theory is a work of fiction.

Teoria's thesis is indebted to the academic works of David Chariandy, Joan Gibson, Leslie Sanders, Christina Sharpe, Rinaldo Walcott. In fact, in most cases the protagonist, Teoria, has used their works liberally, going so far as to intimate co-authorship in the footnote citations. The author thanks these generous relatives for the indulgence. Thank you to Greg Hollingshead for a first reading.

Profound gratitude to my editor Lynn Henry, for all the ways.

Thank you to Sarah Chalfant and Alba Ziegler-Bailey of The Wylie Agency for all the means.

© Jason Chow

DIONNE BRAND's literary credentials are legion. Her book of poetry, *Ossuaries,* won the Griffin Poetry Prize; her nine other volumes of poetry include winners of the Governor General's Literary Award, the Trillium Book Award and the Pat Lowther Memorial Award. Her novel *In Another Place, Not Here* was selected as a *New York Times Book Review* Notable Book and a Best Book by the *Globe and Mail*; *At the Full and Change of the Moon* was selected a Best Book by the *Los Angeles Times* and *What We All Long For* won the Toronto Book Award. In 2006, Brand was awarded the prestigious Harbourfront Festival Prize for her contribution to the world of books and writing, and was Toronto's Poet Laureate from 2009 to 2012. In 2017, she was inducted to the Order of Canada. Brand is a Professor in the School of English and Theatre Studies at the University of Guelph. She lives in Toronto.

A NOTE ON THE TYPE

The body of *Theory* has been set in Farnham. Designed
by Christian Schwartz, based on a typeface by Johannes
Fleischman, a german punchcutter who worked for the
Enschedé Foundry in Haarlem, Holland in the mid-to-
late 1700s. The unusual exuberant angularity make the
type appears so active.